Lily Spender

Godwyn's Ordeal

Vol. I

Lily Spender

Godwyn's Ordeal
Vol. I

ISBN/EAN: 9783337045586

Printed in Europe, USA, Canada, Australia, Japan

Cover: Foto ©Andreas Hilbeck / pixelio.de

More available books at **www.hansebooks.com**

GODWYN'S ORDEAL

BY

MRS. JOHN KENT SPENDER,

AUTHOR OF

"BOTH IN THE WRONG," "MARK WILMER'S REVENGE,"
"PARTED LIVES," "JOCELYN'S MISTAKE,"
"HER OWN FAULT," &c., &c.

> "She, not only through her wit,
> Coud all the feat of wifely homeliness,
> But eke, when that the case requiréd it
> The common profit coudè she redress;
> There nas discórd, rancóur, nor heaviness,
> In all that land that she ne coud appease,
> And wisely bring them all in rest and ease.
> .   .   .   .
> O! needless was she tempted in assay!
> But wedded men ne knowen no mésure
> Whan that they find a patient creatúre."
>
> CHAUCER.

IN THREE VOLUMES.

VOL. I.

LONDON:

HURST AND BLACKETT, PUBLISHERS,

13, GREAT MARLBOROUGH STREET.

1879.

TO

My Five Elder Girls and Boys,

TO WHOM THE FIRST VOLUME OF THIS BOOK

WAS READ AS IT WAS WRITTEN

ON THE SEASHORE DURING

A HAPPY SUMMER HOLIDAY,

THE EARLIER PORTION OF THIS STORY

IS DEDICATED.

CHAPTER I.

THE hot weather was not yet over at Dullerabad. Anglo-Indian society, such as it could boast of, was mostly at the hills. Many of the officers were yet away on leave. The balls and race-meetings, which it had inaugurated on a minor scale, would not commence for some time.

But the dull season was enlivened by an unusual scandal, which not only supplied the pabulum of necessary interest to those who were oppressed by *ennui* as well as fatigue, but proved so exciting as to reward many who had previously complained of the monotony and excessive heat of Dullerabad. This was the trial of an officer who was accused of firing at a brother officer, and who was said by those who believed in that and other statements to be unfit to remain in Her Majesty's Service, if not deserving the sternest sentence which could be adjudged by a court-martial. There were others who thought that the accused officer was the victim of an unjust conspiracy. His friends declared that he was provoked to send a challenge which he was subsequently compelled to withdraw at his peril. They repeated his own statements that he had only afterwards visited his fellow-officer for the purpose of obtaining his signature to a

paper which he took with him, intending
to exonerate himself from dishonourable
imputations; that, though he had loaded
pistols in his pocket, he did not produce
them or attempt to use them, even when
that officer ordered him to leave his house
and called upon his servants to turn him
out, employing opprobrious terms in
English and Hindustani; and that, though
some irregular firing had afterwards taken
place, there had been no blood shed, and
the accuser had been the first assailant.
It was asserted in proof of this that,
though Captain Payton was an expert
marksman, yet at six paces—much less
than the usual duelling distance—he did
not kill, nor even wound, the man whom
he was falsely charged with firing at with
intent to murder.

On the other hand, Payton was known
to be of a violent temper, and the charges

against him were formidable ones. He had nothing but his own assertion to prove the accusations to be false, and having been summoned to attend the first court of inquiry in the mess-room of the regiment, orders had been issued by which he was placed under arrest till the charges against him were framed on the different allegations. News of the approaching court-martial had for days been attracting great attention.

It was no wonder that Dullerabad was in a state of excitement; such a pretty quarrel between two English officers had not been heard of within the memory of man. Even the stolid Sepoys seemed to know that something unusual was going on.

The sound of horses' hoofs and of voices in conversation sometimes penetrated to a darkened room, to which a pale emaciated woman was confined, after giving a new young life to the world under circumstances of such hopeless anguish of mind as well as body that, had not her early religious teaching restrained her, she could have been ready, like Job's wife, to " curse God and die." The windows were open, but no punkah was moving to allay the difficulty of breathing caused by the heat. Only the faithful ayah, who was sitting by her side, and who had refused to leave her mistress during the day or the night, was flapping the flies away from her with the feather trimming of a fan.

It was well for Mrs. Payton that she had never joined other ladies in their railing against the children of the soil. On her first coming out to India she had received the usual warning against the native servants. She had been told that

they were rogues every one of them—
ready to steal before one's very eyes.
But she had acted upon her natural impulse, endeavouring to attach them to
herself. And now this ayah seemed an
angel to her—an angel with a black face.
For most of the English ladies who had
lately given her solemn bows or little
jerky nods of the head had now forsaken
her in her great extremity; and Mrs.
Payton had felt their treatment the more
keenly since she had hitherto been a favourite in the station.

The fame of her beauty and accomplishments had usually preceded her to any
station at which her husband's regiment
was likely to be quartered, and she had
always held her own against the annual
importation of young ladies from England.
Perhaps some of her former rivals were
not likely to be sorrowfully affected by

her sudden reverse of fortune. One or two of the gossiping Englishwomen would have been glad to come and see her, but they were wives of junior officers—her true-hearted friends were at the hills—and she had a natural dread of such voluble visitors.

Poor Mrs. Payton's forsaken and poverty-stricken condition was the more touching because she had always hitherto been apparently in easy circumstances. If her husband were in debt, she was comfortably ignorant of it, but her apartment had now been stripped of almost its necessary articles of furniture. The vultures had descended upon her, and her ruin had been complete.

So utter had been the sudden revelation of her poverty that before the birth of her baby, when she had contended with her weakness, her own delicate fingers had fashioned the scanty little dress of plain black stuff which was worn by her only other child, a little girl about eleven years of age, with wells of hidden feeling in her pale, restrained little face, who sat hour after hour by her mother's side. Why she had made the dress black, Mrs. Payton could hardly have told. It was rather by a subtle instinct than by any reasoning process, just as the mother's prayers, which she had mingled with the laboured stitches and with every painfully-drawn breath, were inarticulate utterances rather than thought-out prayers.

She was past following any connected train of thought now, and no one knew it better than the little Wynnie—Godwyn the child had been called, from her mother's maiden name—who, when the

ayah paused in her fanning, crept up
to her mother and kissed the thin fingers,
as she had often kissed them at intervals
during the weary hours. The touch of the
child's pure lips, cool and soft as a rose-
leaf, on the burning fingers, seemed to stir
the invalid as nothing before had stirred
her, but it did not rouse her even to the
ghost of a smile: she was only roused
again to the prevailing sense of her
misery.

"Is there any news?" she wailed, as
she had wailed a hundred times before;
"tell me, is there any news?"

The tender little mouth quivered, but
habit prevailed, and the child restrained
her tears.

"You know, darling," she said, speaking in a tender, protective way, as if
their natural positions had been inverted,
"the doctor said he would come and

tell you, but that no news could be known yet, not for another month at least."

Mrs. Payton turned wearily on her side, incapable of noticing that the girl, who carried about a woman's heart in a child's body, had, from motives of her own, retailed, parrot-like, the doctor's answer.

Once, during that weary day, little Godwyn had caught a glimpse of the officers marching off with uniforms and swords to the court-martial, a cloud of dust tracking their steps. She had listened for their return; she had in-quired, and she knew that what her mother was waiting for was over.

No one would have had the heart to explain the circumstances to her, or to tell her that the verdict was likely to be

given against her father. Some one had
been unwise enough to say in her presence that it was "an ugly look-out for
poor Payton," and more than once the
sick woman had murmured something
about "disgrace" in a voice which came
in whispers from her lips, though whenever she remembered the presence of her
daughter, she had tried to repress the
occasional shudder which shook her from
head to foot.

Little Godwyn, precocious as she was,
knew nothing of the nature of the offence
or the probable gravity of the sentence, but
she evaded direct answers, and no longer
tried to cheer her unhappy mother or
give a turn to her thoughts, when she
heard her muttering in words which
she did not catch plainly or com-
prehend—

"News—why should I ask for news?

Even if he were acquitted he would never be able to hold up his head again."

CHAPTER II.

FORTUNATELY for the child, though
her intelligence was quick, her education had been imperfect, owing to
her residence in India, and she had but
a very faint conception of the real importance of the matter. She had been ready
enough to credit the statement of the
ayah that her father was suffering from
the jealousy and unkindness of other
officers. It was easy enough to believe
her mother's petulant statement that
these gentlemen had been circulating
untruths about Captain Payton, and that
as they had been slandering him, her

father, who was a proud man, would "never be able to hold up his head again."

The middle-aged, soldier-like surgeon, dressed in plain clothes, and wearing a helmet with a white turban round it, need not therefore have started back at Wynnie's precocious wisdom, when the child, who had lingered at the door of the room, stopped him, and pulled him a little forward, so that she could get a better view of his grave and anxious face, and whispered, tears filling her great eyes as she spoke—

"I know how unfair they have been to poor papa. Don't tell her more than you can help about it—she has been asking all the time—she does nothing but ask, and I—I am so afraid that any news will make her worse."

Godwyn burst into stifled sobs, as instantly controlled again, as she made the announcement of the extent of her knowledge. But there was no look of shame in her innocent, thin, sallow face. Her acquaintance with military law was as limited as her knowledge of the laws of her country, though perhaps she had picked up as much as many women who are supposed to have come to years of discretion know about either. Her whole idea of the misery which had fallen upon her mother was, that other men had been unkind and unjust to her father. She expected the doctor to be as indignant with these oppressors as she was herself. Her bosom heaved with excitement—her eyes, now that the tears were driven back from them, were dilated with pity and anger.

The doctor had understood too well from the first how matters were likely to end with the unfortunate officer.

No one knew better than himself how the character which Payton had always borne in the regiment, of being unnecessarily harsh with his men, and too often overbearing with his fellow-officers, was likely to cause a strong feeling against him. Payton himself had declared that there had been false swearing amongst the witnesses, but it was impossible for an outsider to give an opinion on such a matter. On the contrary, the doctor had seen, only too plainly, as the inquiry had continued, how it would have been better for the accused could it have been closed at an earlier stage, and how his passionate accusations of evil-speaking and perjury, leading to recriminations and contradictions, had only told most disastrously against the unhappy man.

Doctor Rybot could not help being

versed in all the gossip of the station; he therefore knew that it was no wonder that Payton, who had always been liberal to prodigality, and who did not have a farthing with his wife, had not been able to save out of his pay. He understood the tale that was told by the single empty chair by the side of the sick bed, the utter desolation, the piteous dreariness of the place. The Paytons had always been plundered by their servants, and every single article of value had now been taken from the dying woman, though one servant at least—the faithful nurse—would have been willing enough to die for her mistress.

The dying woman! Yes, he knew that she must die—that if there had been any hope of her rallying before, her husband's sentence would prove her death-shock.

" She will die of it, poor thing; it will have killed her; and as to the child—well, there was no hope of saving it before," the kind Doctor thought pitifully as he looked down at her altered face, and remembered how well she had looked in the riding-habit which displayed the fine proportions of her beautiful figure on the handsome chestnut horse—a piece of Payton's extravagance—the first time he had met her near the parade-ground. Under other circumstances he might have felt justified in deceiving her, from the best of motives, but he knew that the verdict would be likely to go against Payton, and that the news would reach her from coarser lips if not from his. It was better for him to break it to her as gently as he could. She opened her eyes as he took the vacant chair, and the altered aspect of the room and its empty condition jarred on her sense of fitness and self-respect, as it had jarred on her once or twice before.

" You see, Doctor Rybot," she repeated almost mechanically, as the courtesy, which was second habit, prompted her to falter—" you see, Doctor Rybot, I was —obliged—to part with the furniture—I could not blame them—poor things— their wages were unpaid—but it will be all right—directly—George returns."

The weak voice trembled as it uttered the last words—words which had unconsciously taken the form of a question, and which made it easier for him to tell her that her husband could not yet return to her—that there were rumours which said he would be degraded from the army, and confined at present by the judgment of the Court.

She read the answer in his eyes.
The terrible idea which she had guessed
at already, and which her heart had
anticipated for hours—which had seemed
to her to be as long as eternity—was
endorsed by the expression of those eyes,
and she hid her face in the pillows in
shame and misery.   Her pride was
utterly broken down in that moment
of intensest anguish.

"The result of the inquiry cannot be
officially announced for a considerable
time," he added, trying to cheer her, and
endeavouring in vain to explain something
about the proceedings having to be re-
viewed by the Commander-in-Chief, and
afterwards sent to England for confirma-
tion.

"Can I do anything for you?" he pitifully inquired, after a pause, as he kept one
hand on her pulse, and with the other took

a sedative from his pocket. But her impulse was to turn from her best friends, and to ask only for darkness and silence, as she rejected the proffered medicine with a momentary irritation.

"God is kind to me," she wailed— "God is kind to me. He will let me die. Doctor, you must not think—I am—a—contemptible coward—but I have not the moral courage—to face the life I should have to live. Life has been too difficult—for me—already. But there—is the story of Calvary; I want to think of it. No, your doses will make no difference—I should die just the same; let me keep my head clear while 1 may."

He did not contradict her, and put the sedative away, sitting patiently by her side.

"How long will it be?" she said, after another pause.

"You have guessed the truth," he

said with emotion. "You are slowly sinking—you may live for another day."

He did not reproach himself for the fact that the ill report which he had allowed her to anticipate had proved her final death shock, for if brought to her more abruptly, with more cruel detail, it would have killed her at once.

He expected the next words.

"My children! oh, my children! Give me my baby!"

"One is already provided for," he said, speaking very gently. "We will put it in your arms—if it will be any comfort to you. But the nurse is doing all she can. The little thing has ceased to suffer. It is sleeping what I think will prove—its final sleep. Believe me, dear lady, it is best."

"Thank God," she murmured with a peculiar smile. "Oh, Doctor, is it wicked to feel as if I understand the mothers who, when they leap into the water, take their little ones in their arms?"

He made no answer, as, according to her wish, the baby, with peace already on its tiny features, except for an occasional convulsive movement, of which he told her it was unconscious, was placed gently in its mother's arms. She smiled again, the same peculiar smile, and said—

"It makes me feel happy. Oh, Doctor, do you remember—I have read my Bible too little, and my memory seems to have gone, but there were words which I used to sing years ago—Handel's music, how 'He gathered the lambs?'"

The kind-hearted man was almost overcome, but he rallied his strength and repeated firmly, with an effort,

"'He shall gather the lambs with

His arm, and gently lead those that are with young.'"

"Thank you," she said, with a sigh of relief. "Let us go to sleep—so, together. Give my love to George, and tell him to keep up—a brave front. He does not deserve—all they say about him."

At that moment a little black-robed figure came tip-toeing to the door, and a bird-like voice, carefully pitched, so as not to disturb the invalid, asked in its half woman-like, half child-like accents—

"May I come in ?"

Mrs. Payton started. Her attitude of peace was disturbed. Strange as it may seem, in the half-comatose condition in which she was at intervals, she had forgotten the existence of the second child, who had so conscientiously remained aloof in an adjoining room, fearing to intrude upon a private conversation.

"Wynnie!" she suddenly cried, in a tone of greater anguish than she had hitherto allowed herself to use. "Oh, Doctor, she is penniless—alone in the world. What can her father do for her? She will only be an encumbrance to him. Oh, there is no one—no one to whom I can entrust my little Godwyn."

The doctor waved the child out of the room, and then asked—

"Have you no relatives?"

"I am an orphan. I have offended my relations. You do not know my story. I made a runaway marriage, and at the time I was engaged to one of the best and tenderest of men—I could not marry him, for I did not love him. If I sinned I am rightly punished."

"Have you no friends in England to whom you can send the child."

"None—without money,"

"Some money must be subscribed at once, and I will head the subscription with a handsome sum," thought Doctor Rybot to himself. "She thinks so badly of the other officers—her mind being naturally prejudiced in favour of her husband—that it will not do to mention it to her. But I feel sure that none of the fellows here will let the little girl suffer."

Aloud he said—

"I will devise some scheme which will be sure to satisfy you. Trust to me. I will look in in an hour's time."

Doctor Rybot went out deep in thought, just as a group of officers, who had been standing together discussing the unusual event at Dullerabad, dispersed to their respective bungalows. A little further on he fell in with a Lieutenant Newland, a friend of the Paytons, who had been absent from the station for a few weeks, and had hurried back at the news of Payton's arrest and his poor wife's premature confinement.

Charlie Newland's face wore an expression of the deepest gloom. If there was one woman whom he admired in the whole of India, after whose model he said he should like to select his own wife, that woman was Mrs. Payton. He often told the story of how when he came out, a shy subaltern, to India, before he belonged to the crack corps on which he prided himself at present, Mrs. Payton had taken pity on his forlorn condition, and how, without patronising the raw youth, who resented secretly the unkind snubbing of some of the other ladies, she had invited him to her house, gradually drawing him out, emboldening him by her gentle and sympathetic manner, till he ac-

quired a self-possession which astonished
himself. He often said that Mrs. Payton
had been "the making" of him. It was
she who had discovered the talents the
existence of which had been unsuspected
even by himself; she who had urged
him on till he had passed in Hindustani,
and was now distinguishing himself by
hard study of military science.

"Oh, confound it! I can't stand it.
Since I have returned from my leave
I am more and more disgusted with
India," said the young fellow, using
stronger language than I can put down
here, when he heard from Doctor Rybot
of the hopeless nature of Nellie Payton's
illness, and felt that there would be a
void in his existence when that gracious
woman was taken away from this earth.

"I don't see that India has anything
at all to do with it. She has simply

made the mistake that many a woman makes, of choosing the wrong man when she had two to choose from," said the less excitable doctor.

"But what a wife she was to him, even when he was in his tantrums! I know poor Payton had a lot to make him nervous, but I must say he used to be the very deuce for heat."

"That reputation has told against him."

"It's unfair that it should. It was very well for Hall, who has a comfortable position and nothing to irritate him, or for Discombe, who hates Payton for what he calls his haughty, patronising manners, to give his opinions about these things. I think I ought to know best. I know that, if he was a little hot, he was good-hearted at the bottom. I know that he was

A 1 where pluck and spirit were wanted. I remember how he charged into that mass of Sikhs and got his regiment out of danger; and I call it monstrously ungrateful," muttered the young fellow sulkily. "Payton has his enemies, and I'll get to the bottom of this matter; but meanwhile there's the wife—a woman in a thousand—every one seems to have forsaken her," added the young man bitterly. "I can't think what these women are made of. I know there's not one of them to hold a candle to her, with her grace and her refinement. Would it—would it be thought strange of me," he asked, as a sudden fit of boldness seized him, "now that they say she is dying, to go and visit her myself, and offer to take care of her child?"

"You would be a young guardian

for her daughter," said the doctor sympathetically, as he wrung Newland's hands. "But I think you need not trouble yourself about appearances. This case is too far gone for any one to make remarks—as to that, I make it a rule in life never to trouble about what people say; and as to the little girl, why it may be a matter of real destitution, and the poor thing may die more happily if some provision is made."

"I have come as fast as I could, directly I heard the news," said Charlie Newland an hour afterwards, when, at his urgent request, he had been admitted to see the dying woman, and felt how hopeless it was for him to try to find words to express his sympathy for her, and his reverence. "Can I do anything for you?" he added presently, unconsciously repeating the very same words which had been used by Dr. Rybot in the like difficult position, and missing the frank, gracious smile which no longer lit up the thin pale face.

"You do not mind one visitor. Do you remember when you used to have quite a levée to see you?" the young man continued, beginning to feel a little nervous, and trying in vain to cheer her up, and to avoid the affair of the disaster.

"I never cared for any of those visitors. I used to be much happier when we were far up country," she answered, and he noticed that she spoke as if in a dream. He noticed also the child which she held in her arms—though, like most young men, he was not much given to noticing infants.

But this one looked so strange, like a piece of wax with closed eyes, and the mother held it strained so closely to her; it somehow reminded him of a marble effigy on one of the tombs in an old cathedral.

She herself, who had been raised for this interview on her pillows, carefully arranged by the faithful ayah with decorous drapery of Indian shawls, had suspected for the last few minutes that the child had ceased to breathe, but said nothing about her suspicion, lest they should take the baby from her. She had long ceased to shiver at these grim reminders of death—the death which was so quickly to claim her as its prey.

The objects which were around seemed to have nothing to do with her, they had already become part of a fleeting

phantasmagoria. It seemed to her that
with the present scene she had no part
or lot; the voices of Charlie Newland,
and of her attentive nurse, seemed to be
very far away from her. They were
sounding to her through a mist, and
already the cold was creeping up her
members. She had never been capable
of much analysis, and had never stopped
te criticise her husband's character. She
was as far as ever from moralising now,
but she felt the influence of Charlie
Newland's courteous and sincere manner.
She knew that, before she admitted him,
she had determined to ask something of
him, but what that something was she
was in danger of forgetting.

Then she made one of the strenuous
efforts not uncommon to the dying.
Husbanding all her little strength, with
glittering eyes, and a deceptive colour

returning to her cheeks, she said hurriedly, speaking for the first time connectedly—

"You ask me how you can help me. I thank you. I made up my mind before you came to ask you to write a letter from my dictation. Can you get pen and paper? Time is precious!"

It so happened that Newland had a pencil-case in his pocket; he tore out some leaves from his pocket-book, and made her understand that whatever she dictated he could copy clearly again.

The letter astonished him. It ran as follows:—

"Friend who behaved so nobly to me, and who forbore even to blame me for one of the greatest wrongs which a woman could inflict on a man, do you wonder that I venture to address you?

Now that I write to you, it is too late
for repentance. God may forgive me,
but I can never atone to you. Such
strange fancies creep into my head now
that I am dying—I cannot help them
—they seem to be put there. It is
impossible for me now to try to unravel
the past, or to think where the wrong
commenced, but I believe it was with
those who urged me to engage myself
to you because you were rich and I a
penniless girl. They could not bridge
over the years between us, and when
George Payton threw his spell over me,
for the first time I knew that I did not
really love you. Was it not better to
make the discovery then than if I had
waited for our marriage? Was it not
better to flee from you, even on the
eve of our wedding-day? I should have
told you all the truth, I should have

trusted to your generosity. But I was always weak, and I had not the courage. Forgive me, for I am dying, and if I sinned I am rightly punished.

"As to my unhappy husband, such utter misery has fallen upon him that you are amply avenged. He fired at an officer, but I believe in self-defence, without wounding or intending to wound, and after that officer had first in a cowardly manner fired at him. His sentence may be a severe one, and he may be driven to desperation. Think of him mercifully if you should ever hear a garbled statement of his story. He has not a penny in the world, and we have one little girl, without even the means of paying for her passage to England. Do you think I am mad? I am going to send her to *you*. I have no one else to send her to in the dear old mother country. Something—out of myself—I cannot tell what it is, seems to whisper to me that for the sake of the love of God you will take pity on my little friendless one. If you cannot bear the sight of her, you will at least send her to school, and in a few years she may support herself as a pupil-teacher. I do not dread this fate for her. Anything will be better than that she should grow up frivolous, like her mother."

The tears, which Charlie Newland had not shed for years, stood in his honest blue eyes as she panted out the concluding broken sentences of this letter. He made no comment, except to ask for the address, and to say, half reproachfully, that she was not to trouble herself about Godwyn's passage, the expense was nothing, and he would take all the arrangements for it on himself.

She was exhausted, now that the effort was over, and could only gasp—

"You will see my husband and get his consent. I think—he will be glad— to be rid—of the child. He was— always wishing—that she had been a boy."

No private communications had passed lately between Payton and his wife. At first the Captain had professed to make light of the inquiry, but since the matter had assumed a more serious aspect, even the Doctor had abstained from carrying messages between the husband and wife, fearing that the unhappy man might unconsciously criminate himself. Payton was not of a disposition to bear misfortune easily. He had tried at first to show a philosophical resignation to the

accusation, but the unexpected turn which
things had taken was, as he said, past his
philosophy.

The last few minutes of consciousness
granted to Nellie Payton were spent
in dictating parting messages to her
husband. She sank, as the Doctor had
expected, towards the close of the next
day, and great sympathy was shown at
Dullerabad when she and her little baby
were laid in one coffin. It is astonishing
how kind we can most of us be to the
dead. Tender messages came in plenty
when they could no longer act as a
balm to Ellen Payton's bleeding heart;
and flowers arrived in numbers as decora-
tions for her funeral when the eyes
which were closed for ever could no
longer be gladdened by them. There
was even a reaction of feeling amongst
the men who had been so ready to take

a severe view of the case of Captain Payton. Some were willing to make excuses for him now, and to pity him for the fit of passion which had produced such disastrous results. The loss of such a wife, owing to the unhappy circumstances, had reduced the wretched man to a state of grief bordering upon insanity.

On appealing to him, Lieutenant Newland found him utterly unreasonable, and so overwhelmed with shame and misery that he declared his intention of changing his name and entering upon an entirely new life, so as to utterly destroy the landmarks between the future and a past which had become—as he said, through the conduct of others—intolerable to him. He asserted his intention of never seeing his child again, adding that for him to see her would only be to load her with his own unmerited disgrace.

Under these circumstances nothing remained but for Newland to act in accordance with Mrs. Payton's wishes. A lady returning to England offered to take charge of the little girl, and the ship which was to take the desolate Godwyn was expected to arrive almost directly after that which had carried her mother's letter.

CHAPTER III.

ABOUT twenty years ago, when these events happened at Dullerabhad, a house—the origin of which was said to be interesting to antiquarians—stood in extensive grounds on the cliff, near the village of Dornton, in Devonshire. There were traces in parts of the house of Elizabethan architecture, and other parts of it were said to be of a still earlier date. It had belonged in past times to a family that proudly dated its origin from Norman robbers, but it had passed, when that family was ruined, in accordance with the Plutocracy *versus*

Aristocracy of this nineteenth century,
to a man whose father had enriched himself as a manufacturer, and who owned
the paper-mills to which the village which
clustered round it had come to owe its
very existence; for the other little
houses with picturesque tiled roofs, and
the thatched cottages which nestled
beneath the cliffs, were now inhabited
almost exclusively by men who worked
at the mills. The fishing trade had
long ceased to flourish at Dornton, the
fishermen having migrated to other places
on the coast where the fish was less
scarce, and where visitors came to in-
crease their profits in summer.

Nobody at that time came to visit Dornton. It was a curiously secluded out-of-the-
world place, forgotten and deserted it
might almost have seemed, except by the
workers at the paper-mills, who had taken

to the cottages which the fishermen had vacated, and the few resident gentry who were within the radius of half-a-dozen miles.

Hence it was that no modern improvements or sanitory precautions had hitherto interfered with the picturesqueness of Dornton. The artist who loved cottages was fortunate if he found it out, for pretty little hovels with angles and peaks, covered with roses and honeysuckles in summer, remained much as they had been within the memory of man, beautiful as to the exterior, but given over to the reign of vermin, and only fit to be habitations for pigs inside. The cottages were built on the ground. Fortunate were the people who had stone flooring, and still more fortunate they whose bones were not racked by rheumatism, and the majority of whose children were spared to them when fever ran a muck amongst the villagers, settling the difficult question of surplus population, and leaving fewer to struggle up and develop into drunken husbands, quarrelsome wives, and immoral sons and daughters. For minor tragedies were constantly being enacted under the smiling blue sky, amidst the roses and honeysuckles of these pretty little hovels, which looked fit to be painted for a pastoral scene in some theatre.

Very beautiful was the home scenery near Dornton. Nothing, in its way, could be more tempting to the eye than the house on the cliffs, with its stone steps reaching down to the shingly beach, adorned with wild creepers in the tangled and luxuriant growth of years. At the back of the house was a river, on the banks of which stood the manufactory.

But even this erection was less unsightly than other buildings of the sort, as the river was in parts exquisitely wooded, and the grey trunks of an extensive avenue of beech trees leading to an old quadrangle screened the paper-mills from view.

Nearly all the profits of this lucrative manufactory accrued to Mr. Bardsley, whose father had not only been the owner, but the projector of the works. And no place of retirement could have suited Mr. Bardsley better. He was generally pronounced to be "a bit of a misanthrope," having experienced some great disappointment earlier in life, though his neighbours were not generally agreed about the nature of this rather vague "disappointment," and only knew that he shut himself up and avoided their society. He scarcely deserved the accusation of misanthropy, since he was still of a kindly, if he had become of an indolent and melancholy, nature. If he took no interest in the growing discontent of the people he employed, it was— to do Mr. Bardsley justice—because he knew nothing of this discontent. No complaints reached him. His fault was that of indifference. For having been educated as a student and taking little active interest in the paper-mills, he preferred to hide himself in solitude since the great grief of his life, amusing himself with his Horace and Plato, or attending to his own garden, and leaving all the management of the works to a hard-working, enterprising man, who had hitherto seemed to prove himself worthy of the trust reposed in him. If this manager had become overbearing and hard in driving bargains with the workpeople, there was no one to tell Mr. Bardsley of the abuse of his confidence. The landed gentry in the neighbourhood were not likely to interfere with him. Mr. Bardsley was a man accustomed to a certain amount of social respect, who had never made failures, and who did not brook interference. He had the character of being exceptional, peculiar and sensitive, as much by natural constitution as by the circumstances of his retired life.

And so Dornton went on without innovations. The old clergyman, who had the tenure of a chapel of ease, and who made but a meagre profit out of his pew-rents, troubled himself but little about the neglected population. Mr. Bardsley was supposed to be a good patron of his, that gentleman declaring himself to be an ardent member of the Church of England, and proving it by renting a goodly number of seats, and usually shirking the going to church. Once only had the Rev. Travers Lewson attempted a feeble remonstrance with Mr. Bardsley as to the neglect of his solemn duties, and had been scornfully told that "he had better look to his own shortcomings before he attempted to meddle with the liberty of other people."

The parson scarcely deserved the remonstrance, for never was a man more inclined to avoid "vain janglings," and "to live peaceably with all men."

"As if I could go through the farce of sitting under his preaching! He gives very good milk for babes, but so diluted that it becomes mere wish-wash for educated people," Mr. Bardsley had fumed to himself, when he wondered "how Lewson could have ventured."

As far as he knew, the spiritual wants

of the poor people were very amply provided for, for Mr. Lewson never meddled
with Dissent, any more than he did with
Ritualism. There was in the village of
Dornton a curious little tabernacle, with its
roof covered with mossy tiles, and slits
for windows—like a toy in a Noah's ark—
and though there was no Methodist
preacher to be the recognised custodian
of the souls which the Church did not see
to, yet an itinerant preacher came to the
little meeting-house about once in the
month, and a few years before there had
been an attempt made to get up a spasmo-
dic revival, which had proved a failure.

With regard to all this, James Bardsley
was like Gallio; he cared nothing. The only
woman who had ever been able to touch
his heart, and whom he forgave in spite of
her ill-treatment of him, had lapsed out
of his life; he heard nothing of her. And

he—a careworn and weary man—as if the
scorching heat of life's afternoon sun had
beat too hardly on his head, and brought
out the wrinkles and white hairs before
their time, shut himself up in the curious
old house, which admirably suited him, by
its antique associations, and by its oak
panels, and coats of arms over the old
mantelpieces. Outsiders knew little more
about the house than that the door opened
on a cheerful carpeted hall, garnished
with pictures and statuary, in accordance with its owner's artistic tastes.
But one wing, at least, was unfurnished, and given over to owls and bats.
For what could a solitary bachelor do
with such a place? During a great part
of the year he was said to wander like
a ghost amongst the towering trees, or
by the usually silent walls, which gave
back whispering echoes. For all appear-

ance of life the house might not have been inhabited at all. The great gates in front of the quadrangle, which communicated with the avenue, were always kept closed, and Mr. Bardsley himself slipped out through a side-door when he visited the village.

People pitied him, but they need not have done so. His servants were devoted to him. For a great part of the year the domestic management, about which he was seldom consulted, had run with perfect ease on well-oiled wheels, the reins being held with a light hand by the old housekeeper, who had lived with him ever since the death of his father.

There was only one emergency for which Betsy and her band of handmaids were not found to be fully competent, and that was the holiday time, when the usual peaceable routine of Dornton manor-house was somewhat rudely interrupted by the advent of Mr. Bardsley's nephew, the son of a favourite sister, long since dead, whom the old man had adopted. It was no secret that Mr. Bardsley had made Humphrey Carleton his heir, the boy's father having married again, and being glad enough, now that he was hampered with another family by his second wife, to hand Humphrey over to the brother-in-law, who had promised to let the boy inherit all the profits of his lucrative business on condition that he should take the name of Bardsley.

Humphrey, who was at this time at the noisy age of fourteen, and who was at Rugby during term-time, spent his holidays at Dornton, often asking to bring with him one of his schoolfellows, and making the neighbourhood too hot to hold him in consequence of his numerous exploits. The heavy damages which Mr. Bardsley had been called upon to pay for the supposed injury inflicted upon poultry and pigs in consequence of Humphrey's fancy for hunting them with dogs, were nothing to the danger incurred by the really valuable art treasures with which the habitable part of the manor-house was somewhat profusely decorated.

Betsy's coaxings and entreaties had been found so useless on former occasions, that now that the Christmas holidays were drawing near, Mr. Bardsley had recourse to an expedient which he had lately adopted, when necessity was pressing, of inviting a maiden sister to come and stay with him during the vacations, and help him to keep an eye on his nephew and his pranks.

Aunt Rachel was already ensconced at

the manor-house, three weeks before
the time, under the specious excuse that
it was necessary for her to be there to
see to the removal of the valuable china,
which was usually laden upon velvet
brackets or exposed in glass cupboards,
to suit Mr. Bardsley's artistic fancy, and
which would be likely enough to be frac-
tured by the rebounding of the scape-
grace's hard balls.

The good lady—who disapproved of
the manor household altogether, who
subscribed to two missionary societies,
yet never thought of improving the condition of the Dornton heathen, and who
only condescended to help her brother
because she had no objection to the
change of air and the good living at the
manor-house, but whose opinion it was
that James was doing his best to ruin
his nephew—was deeply engrossed by

the tiresome task of fitting, with Betsy's assistance, the brown holland pinafores, which had been washed, and had consequently lost their shapes, on the rich tapestry-covered furniture of the drawing-room, when she was interrupted by Mr. Bardsley. She noticed that his usually calm appearance had been strangely ruffled, and that though he was generally reticent to a fault, he did not attempt to hide the expression of emotion on his face.

"More trouble about that boy!" thought Rachel, as she desisted from her task, unwillingly sending the housekeeper away, and preparing herself to listen to James's fresh difficulty. "I should think fifty per cent. better of the masters if they would flog more of the mischief out of the young rascal."

But Mr. Bardsley had no announce-

ment to make about Humphrey. Whatever he had to say, it moved him so
greatly that he had to sit down and to
essay once or twice to speak before he
could get out the words.

" I have heard," he said at last, " from
poor Ellen Payton. Her letter is a touching one, written when she was dying.
What struggles and trials the poor
creature must have passed through before
she could abase her woman's pride to
write such a letter to me !"

He turned away in irrepressible emotion, nor was it strange that Rachel could
make no answer. Hitherto the story of
Ellen Godwyn's faithlessness had been
the skeleton in the closet, never men-
tioned between Mr. Bardsley and his
nearest relations. It was to be expected
that the first time that name passed
James Bardsley's lips, the strong man

should be pale with a pallor almost livid.

But the pause was prolonged. Rachel did not encourage him to continue. She had her own ideas and ways, strongly defined on many subjects, as most maiden ladies had in the days before people talked much about the disabilities of women. Rachel was not conscious of any " disabilities," her heart was guarded by its brass of " principle," like a coat of mail armour, against all conduct that was foolish. She had strongly disapproved of Ellen Godwyn in her girlhood, and death and trouble made no difference to this disapproval.

The pause lasted till James Bardsley was compelled to turn his face to where Rachel stood, a living mark of exclamation. He was disconcerted. On the receipt of the unexpected letter he had at first been agitated by strangely conflicting feelings; but then, after locking himself for a time into the little room he called his " den," and looking at the dead past in a different light from that in which he had looked at it before, he had come down to Rachel a softened and altered man, all the tender generosity latent in his nature finding scope in the thought of receiving and welcoming the friendless little waif. How should he break the news to Rachel when she had that expression in her face? He wished that he had never invited her, as he beat about the bush, saying,

" She seems to have had a strangely unhappy life."

" What else could she expect? a poor disgraced creature," said Rachel, breaking silence, her words jarring on him. " I'm sure her conduct was the talk of

the country round, running away on the
night before her marriage with a man
she knew nothing about, who might
have had half-a-dozen other wives!
Whatever she suffered, James, she
brought it on herself. People generally
have to bear the consequences of their
own folly."

"Rachel, she is in God's hands," he
answered with an irrepressible groan, trying to hide from her how he was almost
writhing at her unnecessary allusions.
"You may spare her your reproaches
—her heart returned to me at last. As
a proof of it, she has confided her only
child to my care."

"Proof of it indeed! when she played
fast and loose with you!" cried Rachel,
indignant for her brother. "Does it
mean that the father who deprived you
of your wife cannot manage to keep his

own child? James, it is just the way with people who go wrong to try to shift their burdens on the shoulders of other people. I would allow Mr. Payton to reap what he has sown."

He shifted his attitude uneasily. His was a sensitive nature, and he hated a war of words, but having begun this conversation he was bound to express his resolution.

"I have up my mind to take the child," he said. "I have promised that Humphrey shall be my heir, and of course I shall not go back from my promise, but I shall bring this little girl up as if she were my own. She is alone in the world. There are circumstances, which I cannot explain, about the father. I am getting an oldish man now, Rachel, and how can I expect God to forgive me if I cherish revenge against George Payton

now that misfortune is heavy upon him?
—how heavy I cannot tell you."

There was another painful pause, only
broken by Rachel fidgeting with the
strings which tied the covering of an
ottoman. She had never heard her
brother speak in this way before, and
had a sense of discomfiture which was
new to her. Yet, as she stooped to hide
her face, she could not help muttering
rather curiously,

"I doubt the wisdom of keeping the
child in igorance of these — circumstances."

He turned like an animal at bay, facing
her with determination.

" Of course you will not be so insane
as to tell her anything about the history
either of her father or her mother. Your
heart did not speak there, Rachel. You
would not be so cruelly hard as to hang

a weight round the young girl's neck. Let her come here, and be happy, innocent, and free."

And he left his astonished sister, not only discomfited, but with a vague sort of compunction.

CHAPTER IV.

IT was remarked that James Bardsley seemed to be a different man from the day that little Godwyn was expected at the manor-house. He took the housekeeper into his further confidence, rather than his sister, and with Betsy's assistance prepared one of the prettiest rooms for the child, engaging a young woman from the village to wait upon her in the capacity of nurse. Nothing would satisfy him but he must go himself to meet the coach, which stopped a few miles away from the simple village, which was at present undisturbed by the thunder

of a train or the scream of a whistle.
When a line of railway was first of all
continued to a neighbouring town—which
seemed to the simple villagers as grand
as a metropolis—though it was in reality
but a small and unimportant place, only
accommodated with a waiting-shed and a
ticket-office, the Dornton people used to
walk out to see the sight of rushing trains
and hissing engines, like "ramping and
roaring lions." But this excitement had
ceased now, and the Dornton folk
declared themselves better satisfied with
the coach, which had been driven for
years by the same old coachman, who was
garrulous and autocratic.

He was particularly lazy and out of
temper, when one evening, early in
December, the coach arrived later than
usual in a drizzling rain, and the different
boxes had to be discovered by the aid of a

dim lantern. Mr. Bardsley was so much
of a stranger—having for so many years
confined himself to the precincts of his
own village, except for an occasional visit
to London—that the coachman was recalled to a sense of politeness by suddenly recognizing him just as a weak
little voice emanated from the interior of
the coach, and a child, covered with
numerous wraps, was handed out amongst
the boxes. Her new guardian caught a
glimpse of a poor little white, pinched
face, and was conscious of a feeling of
disappointment as the little girl gave a
pant of fright when he came forward
eagerly to claim her. The scene was so
new to her, and all the faces were so
strange; the cold had penetrated to her
very bones, and the sensation was so uncomfortable of being handed from a coach
as if she were just like a bale of goods,

that she might have been forgiven if she
had indulged, as many children would
have done, in convulsive sobs, instead of
the emotion which forced itself out in that
one great pant.

"Don't be frightened of me, my dear,"
said a voice, which spoke more kindly to
her than the voices of the busy people
who had sometimes jostled her during the
voyage; and indeed Mr. Bardsley's tone
could not have been gentler had it been
that of a woman, so touched was he
by the sufferings of the little lonely
child.

She had heard of Dornton as of a bleak
place, cold and miserable after India,
and it seemed like a dream of fairyland,
or some exquisite childish pantomime, to
be introduced to the pretty bedroom,
adorned with pink draperies, with bunches
of roses on the wall, and soft green

mosses on the velvet carpet—altogether contrary to the sternest canons of art, but a miracle of beauty to Godwyn's tired eyes. Betsy had lit the waxen candles when they descended to the sitting-room. A large cheery-looking fire was burning on the hearth, and Aunt Rachel sat, rigid and impenetrable, at the tea-table. She did not frown, but most certainly she did not smile.

"You give her a very warm welcome, to be sure," said James Bardsley, deprecatingly, with suppressed indignation, and those words reminded Rachel that the thing was real. She did not mean to be unkind, and she roused herself to the emergency.

So this was Ellen's child; not much like Ellen Godwyn as Rachel remembered her, with the glory of brilliant colouring which had distinguished her in youth.

Rachel had unconsciously pictured the
child like the little one who was sent to
Silas Marner, with those exquisite daffodil
lights in the golden glory of the hair
which are never seen but in the hair of
young children. But Wynnie's hair was
nut-coloured, and there was a dread experience of the bitterness of life in her
large, suffering eyes— brown, with a hazel
brown like the eyes of a young gazelle,
and strangely deep with an unnatural
expression. The face was not only pale
and pinched, but sallow, with the peculiar
sallowness common to most people kept
too long in India, and the little hands,
which were tightly locked together, were
unnaturally thin and sharp in outline,
whilst the lines of the long black dress—
the same dress which Nelly Payton's weak
fingers had fashioned for her, and which
Charlie Newland had afterwards had

plentifully covered with crape — fell straight and stiff round the little figure.

" What a queer-looking child !" thought Rachel, wonderingly, not knowing that poor Godwyn was looking queerer than usual.

The sudden change of scene after the long, fatiguing journey, the hot atmosphere after the intense cold, and the excitement of meeting her new guardian, had proved too much for the weak, nervous system of the motherless little waif. Wynnie made one useless effort to raise the hot cup of tea which Miss Bardsley had given her to her lips, then the table swam, the floor began to sink, a dozen windows took the place of the three, the lights appeared to vanish, and darkness closed around her.

" Water ! cold water, James ! You

give her no chance if you hug her up like that. Here, let me have her; undo her dress!" cried Rachel, whose sympathies were moved by the sudden attack of faintness. But to her astonishment James Bardsley was already, with tender touch, unloosing the little frock himself, "for all the world," as Rachel afterwards remarked when she told the story, "as if he had been an old nurse."

Some such thoughts as those which haunted poor Charles Lamb when he composed that most pathetic piece of prose-poetry, "Dream Children," passed through James Bardsley's mind when, after a few moments, the child—whom Rachel was now ready to take from him —opened her eyes with a sigh of relief, and nestled closer to him, remaining perfectly still, as if she had found an asylum which suited her, with a strange content.

"She is only exhausted—she wants food and rest," said Rachel, astonished at the sort of freemasonry which seemed to be so easily established between the two. James had never before been known to notice children, and certainly this girl was not much like his lost love. Rachel could not guess what subtle and remote likenesses of voice and expression, un-noticed by herself, the man had already been able to trace in this pale little creature.

"At any rate she does not favour her father," he had more than once said to himself. It was well he was spared this. Perhaps he would not have been able to bear it had there been a strong likeness to George Payton. For the night Godwyn was handed over to Betsy, who seemed to have a natural capacity and handiness about children, and who was thankful to have an outlet for this capacity without the bullying to which she was subjected by Master Humphrey.

And in the morning, when Rachel came down, rather later than usual, she was mortified to find that her brother's tea had been already poured out for him by the little new-comer, and that, her breakfast being concluded, Wynnie was already nestling in her guardian's arms and burying her little pale face on his shoulder.

"Oh!" she said, with a sublime air of self-abnegation, when her brother asked her for a second cup, "*I* have done with the tea; you can let the child pour it out for you in future!"

It was just the fuss about trifles which James Bardsley disliked. He showed his vexation in his manner, and the child, with the precocious penetration which made her immediately perceive that something was amiss, slipped quietly off his knees and went to rejoin Betsy and the little maid who had been engaged to wait upon her.

"You will make the girl ridiculous if you go on with her in this way!"

"It was my fault for stroking her hair and taking her on my knee. I am old enough to be her grandfather, and I have told her to call me uncle."

"Uncle!" exclaimed Rachel, with a peculiar intonation; "she will know you are not her uncle."

"And why on earth should she know it?" asked Bardsley, a little sternly.

It was soon understood that little Wynnie Payton was to be treated as if

she were Mr. Bardsley's niece. Betsy
received strict orders not to undeceive
her on this point. The question of a
governess was next mooted, but here
Mr. Bardsley was again authoritative.
He summoned a doctor from a neighbouring town to come to his assistance, and
the doctor gave it as his advice that
there should be scarcely any lessons,
plenty of fresh air, and plenty of indul-
gence.

"The best thing in the world for her
will be the bracing air of your moors
and the salt breezes of the sea. If you
want her to live to grow up, let her
have her fill of them," said the kindly
doctor, whose opinion tallied with Mr.
Bardsley's.

And both of them proved right. For
the child, who at first had been constantly grieving quietly in a distressful

manner, left off cowering under the bed-
clothes at night, and muttering her
mother's name in a piteous way in her
dreams. Restorative sleep came to her
by degrees, though Betsy was not always
a wise companion for her, in spite of her
excellent nursing and her capable fingers.
And though in those December nights,
before Humphrey returned for his holidays, a cold thrill had often run through
the sensitive child's veins as the old
woman humoured her fancy by telling
her stories of supernatural appearances,
while the wind was shrieking through
the branches of the trees in the garden,
and the girl crouched with shivering feelings before the fire which the servant had
heaped up in the large kitchen-chimney,
yet little Godwyn showed her unusual
precocity by being careful not to intrude
herself on Miss Bardsley for society, and

preferring to be content with that of the servants.

"Uncle," she had been told to call Mr. Bardsley. Rachel had been put to silence, and yet there was something indefinable in her manner to the girl, which made Godwyn at once aware of some difference in her position. She accepted that difference and made the best of it, preparing to put up with Humphrey's teasing. Was he not the heir? a handsome and noble boy, as Betsy had informed her, and she a little desolate woman-child, whose father somehow did not write to her—with only her innocence and her youth? From the first she was prepared to give way to the boy.

"Master Humphrey was in no way bound to put up with her," Rachel had puzzled her by explaining; "he could not be expected to put up with a girl's vagaries when all the money was to come to him."

Humphrey himself had been annoyed to hear that there was a girl at home this Christmas, and that he could not be allowed to invite one of his usual playmates because she was so delicate. He had intended to call her " Cry Baby," but the tears did not come readily when he made fun of her, and he found the nickname inapplicable. Like his uncle, the noisy boy was sufficiently kind-hearted, and there was something in this thin slip of a girl—who looked so sorrowful, yet managed to keep back her tears— which appealed to the incipient manhood in him, and made him pitiful to her from the first. It was the more wonderful how the children took to each other, since it was quoted as one of

Humphrey's misdemeanours that he had hitherto delighted in badgering girls.

"He has no one else to play with," remarked Aunt Rachel, wonderingly, when she found that her nephew was not only forbearing towards Godwyn Payton, but that he had a hankering fancy for her, and succeeded in bullying her into being his playmate.

"His treatment will be too rough for her," said James Bardsley, shaking his head.

Yet he too became less anxious when it was found that, in company with his new companion, the boy got into fewer scrapes than on the previous holidays. The strangely assorted couple would be absent for hours, whilst Godwyn, thick-booted and wrapped in fur and sealskin, came to no harm from the keen winds which blew on moor or heath, but gained, as the doctor had prophesied, new colour in her pale cheeks, and new brightness in her hazel eyes, till James, with a pang of that pain which is akin to pleasure, discovered fresh likenesses to her dead mother.

" Don't interfere with the children; Humphrey has never given you so little trouble," he would say to Rachel as he " pottered about," as the boy called it, to see that they had everything for their little pleasures.

On Christmas Eve it was decided that they should help the old gardener in putting up a few evergreens in the unsightly chapel of ease. This was Godwyn's idea. Nor could she be satisfied till the children had been remembered, and a neighbouring dame-school transmogrified with pink calico and pretty evergreens. Never before had there been such doings at Dornton, but then never had there been a woman-child to think of them.

Humphrey was almost as pleased as Wynnie. But after he had been working hard for a part of the afternoon, the spirit of mischief which had so long been latent in him, suddenly broke forth. Whilst Godwyn was still buried amongst the evergreens, with her back turned to the door of the chapel, which was called the church, after the gardener had left them, a sudden inspiration came to him. For the fun of the thing he instantly carried it out, turning the key of the door and locking the little worker in. In a few minutes he intended to return and set her free, but something else attracted his attention, and boy-like, he forgot her.

There was a burial-ground close to the ugly church, which would be pretty enough when Spring came, with the trees in full foliage, and the birds singing their epithalamiums to the peaceful dead. But Godwyn had peculiar associations connected with this graveyard. She had sometimes visited it with the little maid, Jane, who had been engaged to take care of her, in the first days of her mourning, before Humphrey came to Dornton, when there had been a strange love of loneliness about the child's unusual sorrow, and when she had an idea that Miss Bardsley liked her to leave the room as soon as she entered it.

She had connected this churchyard with thoughts of the dead mother whom she had left buried beneath the hot Indian sun in the soil of a foreign country. But she also connected it with the new superstitious dread caused by the venom instilled into her by Betsy's stories. The light was already waning when Humphrey shut her in.

As soon as she found that the door was locked, she flung her arms up and gave a sharp cry of horror, but no passer-by noticed it. It might have been one of the owls hooting in the churchyard; no one thought of a little girl locked in, in the darkness, kneeling on the cold flags and beating against the door with her fists in an agony of apprehension.

How the time passed, whether in the flesh or out of the flesh, she could never afterwards tell. She fell down against the door in a state of semi-unconsciousness, which saved her from the terrible sensation of being left alone, with something mysterious in the darkness—something horribly contrary to human nature, which made her blood creep and her hair stand up on her head.

So Humphrey found her, when he suddenly recollected her, more than an hour afterwards, and ran to rescue her, panting and out of breath. The boy was a good deal scared when he saw her lying still, apparently without vitality or power to move.

"No, *I'm* not frightened at anything, you know," he said, trying to get her to laugh as soon as he could make her speak. "As to ghosts and spirits, that's all nonsense; there's only ourselves. Why, of course you're exhausted—that's the reason you were faint. It's the grub or the tuck, or whatever else you like to call it, that's wanted. It *can't* be the darkness. It was a beastly shame to forget you for an hour, I know, but it's not possible that any one—not even a girl—could be hurt by such a thing as that," he added scornfully.

Thus half-wheedling and half-scolding he managed to get his playmate home, his conscience rebuking him not a little when the doctor had to be sent for again the next morning, and when he said that the child was suffering from a curious over-nervous state of excitement.

CHAPTER V.

THE healthy, hearty, joyous lad proved to be the best possible companion for the little weak, over-nervous girl. The episode of Christmas Eve only drew them the closer together. Honest Humphrey thought it right to make a confession to his uncle, but he never forgot that Godwyn made no complaint of his conduct.

"I am awfully sorry for you," he said, touching her more gingerly than he had touched her before, and eyeing her as if she were a sort of natural curiosity, when she was allowed to walk about with him again after her nervous attack. "It was queer, but I'm awfully sorry, and it was so jolly of you not to peach."

For a little while he took her under his protection, and treated her as if she were china, and likely to crack.

But Godwyn's attack had only been transient; she had speedily recovered from it. Her bodily state had steadily improved ever since she had been acquainted with her so-called cousin, and her grief, which had been much less easily forgotten than if it could have been wept out in April tears, like the short-lived griefs of most children, was beginning to be a little healed by the progress of time.

Already, with her passionate, clinging affection, she was beginning to be a fervent worshipper of the riotous boy.

She had languished, since her mother's death, for want of an idol to admire, but Humphrey had supplied the want. An approving smile or a kindly look from the boy would furnish her with happiness for the whole day. He knew that she was his devoted slave, that she would follow him everywhere, even into danger, and the result was that he wished her to be acquainted with his sports.

It so happened that the river was frozen over that Christmas, making an unusual pleasure for the villagers, with whom time had crawled in their dull mill-work, and who had much toil but little amusement in their lives. It was a fine time for the village lads, most of all for Mr. Bardsley's heir, who was a proficient skater, and delighted in the exercise. The delight of walking with

little high-heeled boots on the river—
which she had so admired when she
first came for its flitting shadows and
silvery gleam—was much less to the
delicate Indian child, who suffered from
the cold of the English winter, than to
the hardily-trained boy.

"Why, you have your woollen veil,
your muff, and your furs," said Humphrey indignantly when she objected;
"the cold can't even get to the tip of
your nose. It isn't like you to make
a fuss about nothing. Most girls would
have blabbed about that accident at
the church, but not you—you were
never a sneak. I call it selfish to
object to coming with me to skate."

Godwyn's lip trembled a little at the
opprobrious term "selfish." Humphrey
knew it was more efficacious than any
other sarcastic epithet, and therefore

reserved it for a missile to be flung on special occasions.

"That 'ere boy is at 'is tricks agen, he be," commented one of the villagers, as the "little wench" was seen following Humphrey, who cut figures whereever the ice was thinnest, and otherwise indulged in dangerous exploits, heedless of warnings, with Godwyn sticking as close to him as if she had been his shadow. The natural consequence followed, and when both children were capsized, and had a ducking in the river, none of the men were much surprised, though a few of them who bore a grudge against Mr. Bardsley looked surlily on and did not offer assistance. Humphrey scrambled out again directly, but before he could help the little girl, whose constitution was much more likely to be injured by the serious shock of immersion in the

cruelly cold water, a rough, shock-headed
lad who worked at the manufactory, and
who bore an ill reputation in the neighbourhood, dashed into the river before
him, and, diving like an otter, appeared
with the child safely in his arms, carrying her into a neighbouring cottage.
Humphrey followed him, chopfallen and
with chattering teeth, only to be roughly
pushed from the door that the boy's
mother might the better use her rude
appliances for Godwyn's recovery.

It was a new experience to stand on
the threshold of the old cottage,
shivering and excluded, and yet to
dread returning home for fear of
encountering Mr. Bardsley's just anger.
Humphrey had heard sufficient of the
gossip from Betsy to know, too, that
Ned Carslake (who had rescued Godwyn from the river) was looked upon

as one of the most unpromising boys in the neighbourhood, that the mother, a woman of violent passions, was dreaded as a sort of witch by her poor uneducated neighbours, and that all the Carslakes belonged to an ill-conditioned set, who hated his uncle for his supposed neglect and oppression of the poor. Carslake, father, looked miserable enough when little Godwyn first opened her eyes in the dirty cottage, and beheld him stooping helplessly over her, looking like a wrinkled child, old, grey, and rugged, with the appearance of having aged rather from hard living and endurance than the flight of time. Godwyn vaguely wondered why he held his pipe in his mouth and why he wore a nightcap on his head in the daytime, made out of the leg of an old stocking. Carslake, mother, was a filthy

old crone, certainly repulsive enough
for the received notion of a witch, but
looking as keen as her husband was
vacant, with a short pipe also in *her*
mouth, which she only removed now
and then when it was necessary for
her to do something to the fire which
was being made up for the sake of
the little girl so lately rescued from
drowning. The matted ends of Mrs.
Carslake's hair overhung her quick black
eyes. She was evidently angry from the
way in which she threw the logs on
the hearth, and was saying to her
son,

"It weren't no business o' yourn, lad;
better tew let her be—what call had ye
tew meddle wi' what did na concarn ye?
Ye'll be treated like a dawg for it. Curse
'em all, I ses!"

"Can't you give up the old tune for

to-day, mother?" said the shock-headed lad, who was leaning, dirty, like the rest of the inhabitants of the cottage, against the greasy wall. "Th' wench has come tew—that's thanks enough."

Further converse was interrupted by the entrance of Rachel Bardsley, who had been alarmed by the news of the catastrophe, and had brought the carriage to take the invalid with all care to the manor-house. It would have been over-conscientious, as Miss Rachel said, for her to pretend to love Godwyn Payton as if she were really of the same blood as herself. But the child had endeared herself to the maiden lady, and Rachel was ready with such thanks as she had to the lad who had shown such promptitude in rescuing her supposed niece from the water. All might have ended well, but that she could not help commenting a little curiously on the plentiful store of wood which was being heaped on the fire, and which she knew must have been stolen from the manor-house property.

" How is it you are able to purchase wood in this quantity? It seems to me you are more fortunate than your neighbours, Mother Carslake," said Rachel, as she offered money to the son, which was abruptly declined.

" Heer her! as if the A'mighty did na make His trees grew for the poor as well as for the rich—and as if when a bit of a branch happens to blew down of its own accord, it's to be grudged to them as wishes to keep the rheumatiz fro' their bones," burst out Mrs. Carslake with a storm of curses, which made Rachel glad to get frightened Godwyn safely out of the house.

" Of all the filthy, disgusting old hags !
Wynnie, you must never go near her
again. It will never do, on account of
Humphrey's carelessness, to let these low
people be too familiar with you," said
Aunt Rachel, greatly disturbed, and was
a little surprised when the child answered
her, with wisdom beyond her years,

" It's their way, perhaps, Miss Rachel.
Perhaps no one has taught them
better."

CHAPTER VI.

IT was no wonder that Godwyn had a feverish cold after her ducking in the river; and Mr. Bardsley, who had been congratulating himself on the child's improved appearance, the consequence of her improved health, was considerably fretted when his favourite was ill. Humphrey naturally came in for a large share of his displeasure, his uncle telling him severely that he rejoiced to think the Christmas vacation was so nearly over, and that he would have no further opportunity of injuring his cousin by his freaks. For " cousins " the children had been dubbed from the first, and, if Humphrey suspected the pleasant fiction, he did not resent it.

During the boy's absence in term-time the household collapsed into its normal condition. Aunt Rachel would have been willing enough to prolong her visit, under pretext of looking after the little girl who had come to stay with her brother; but Mr. Bardsley, discovering that Wynnie was dull in Aunt Rachel's presence, and being somewhat afraid of that lady's ideas as a disciplinarian, made an excuse for his sister to visit some of her other relations, without giving any hint of his desire to be rid of her.

After this, Godwyn was allowed to run wild in her own fashion. She soon proved herself to have been an apt pupil of Humphrey by her roving propensities and her objection to the usual toys

supposed to amuse little girls. She
objected to the doll with frizzled hair
and pearl necklace, dressed up like a lady
going to a ball, and much preferred an
ugly old wooden hack, which had con-
soled her in her loneliness in the passage
from India. But both dolls were abandoned after her friendship for Humphrey,
and instead of playing with toys in the
drawing-room she took to practising impromptu cooking in the kitchen, taking
the poultry-yard under her protection, and
spilling the ink in her attempts to write
in her uncle's library.

Everything would have been wrong
according to Rachel's notions of discipline, from the fact that the child was
fed with indigestible niceties at the old
man's late dinner, to the sitting at his
feet on a comfortable rug in the sanctum
which she had dared to invade, and in

which she now installed herself to her own satisfaction whenever she pleased.

But the walks would have been considered the most unconventional of all— the long wild rambles when she coaxed her little maid to accompany her in visits to the villagers, and in which she indulged in long talks with the discontented workpeople, whose colloquial incorrectness would have shocked any careful governess, and was rapidly infecting Godwyn's own style of talk. If they had a morning finer than usual, there was no place so attractive as the beach, with its brown sands glistening and dazzling like gold, and its distant waves, shot blue and green, like the colouring of a peacock; whilst on the darker winter days there was the refuge of Mr. Bardsley's study.

Nothing could be much prettier than

the child's love and enthusiasm for her somewhat eccentric but intellectual benefactor, and the sense of companionship blended with veneration—one of the most exquisite sentiments of human nature—which made her delight to sit quietly for the hour together in the old man's sanctum, looking at him now and then with worshipping eyes.

Mr. Bardsley got used, after a short time, to the pat of the heel of the little boot on the gravel outside his window, and to the childish voice, which said entreatingly—

" Please may I come in ?"

He had been afraid lest she should be bored at first, but he was now accustomed to see the light of his reading-lamp flickering on her glossy hair, and on the large dark eyes, full of grave thoughts.

" What are you doing ?" he would ask
at first; and she would answer,

" I am thinking."

" Thinking" she called it, but it was only
dreaming, and by degrees it dawned on
him that it might be as well for him to
vary her thinking.

He had few books in his library to
tempt a child. But he offered her a copy of
Shakspeare, and she took to it, as he said,
" as naturally as a duck takes to water."

Anything that might have harmed her
slid as easily from her mind as drops of
water from the typical duck's back, as
she sat for evenings together engrossed
over its pages, while its perfection satisfied her unconscious cravings and
appealed to her artistic insight. Mr.
Bardsley would have been disappointed
could he have guessed that she remembered only the intellectual ideas which

took root in her *heart*. As it was, the
phenomenon of so young a girl appre-
ciating Shakspeare delighted him. He
began to look upon Godwyn as a youthful
prodigy; the more so, that though she
had never been taught to sing, now that
the first keenness of her sorrow had
passed away she was continually singing
about the house, and he was musician
enough to admire the sweet inarticulate
music of her songs.

Mr. Bardsley was so contented with
this strangely satisfying new life, that he
was greatly inclined to be jealous of
Humphrey when the lad returned for his
Easter holidays, just as the sticky buds
were appearing on the horse-chestnut
trees and the hedgerows were beginning
to be covered with crumpled leaves. For
again there were wild wanderings on
moor and beach, to watch the flux and

reflux of the advancing tide, or search for primroses, anemones and rare orchids in the woods.

Nothing would satisfy the boy but that Godwyn must join him in his fishing expeditions, and the little girl, nothing loath, had to leap so many streams in fetching Humphrey's fishing-tackle, or running errands for him, that in a short time most of the articles of her limited wardrobe were in the hands of the washerwoman, and Godwyn, as well pleased as ever, ran about in her nurse's baggy stockings.

Mr. Bardsley was puzzled and once more at the end of his resources, when Humphrey, in his attempts to measure a part of the river which he had been told was deep enough to drown a man, overbalanced himself, and frightened his companion half out of her senses. The close of the Easter holidays put a termination again for a time to the old man's worries. But a new source of annoyance showed itself—Godwyn pined after her companion. Nature, as we are told, abhors a vacuum, and the vacuum in the child's new matter-of-fact life having been speedily filled by Humphrey, the difficulty was now to find some one else who should save her from the returning sadness.

A little girl was selected from the village and allowed to play with her. But, as usual, there was no one to fight against open ditches and the constant recurrence of typhoid fever in Dornton. Godwyn attached herself quickly to Matty Morrison, but one week her new friend did not appear, and some excuse was manufactured for her non-appearance. The fever was worse than usual. But Godwyn heard nothing of the prevailing epidemic, till one day when she saw the housekeeper in tears.

Then Godwyn's pent-up feelings burst forth.

"Oh, Betsy! I do love Matty so much —and I know you are hiding it from me —I know she is dying. Oh, Betsy! take me to see her; if you don't I must go with Jane."

"Miss, it is not a fit place for you to go to," said the cautious Betsy, drying her tears. "Your uncle would forbid it—it is not to be thought of."

"If it is not fit for me it is not fit for Matty."

"She is only a common little girl."

"Common, Betsy? didn't God make her?"

"La! Miss, you take one up so sharp

—as if you didn't understand what I meant!"

But the precocious child understood her only too well. Betsy's weak attempt at preventing her did not affect her in the least; with Jane's assistance, she managed to pay her visit to the cottage.

What she saw there moved her in no slight degree. She was trembling strangely when she came in, and stretching her hands towards the fire as if she were cold. When Betsy came to her, she answered, with a shudder which shook her from head to foot, that if the poor children in the village could suffer so much, it was surely little enough for *her* to know of it. And that night she woke again out of her dreams with the old troubled cry—and again the horrible chilling fancies, which had assailed her after her mother's death, seemed to seize upon her heart with a hand of ice.

Betsy had determined to tell Mr. Bardsley. But the strange child anticipated her. She crept into her so-called uncle's study the following morning, and in a low, awe-struck tone gave a description of what was going on at Dornton.

His first thought was one of indignation and alarm that she should have been allowed to venture near the village when fever was raging there; his second, that modern scientific research had proved typhoid fever not to be infectious; his third, to answer as he did,

" Well, I am sorry you have heard about it, my dear; it's not fit for your young ears, and of course it is a very bad business. But you know, if there were no fevers, no wars, or anything sad, the world would be too full of human beings."

Had he not been taken so thoroughly by surprise he would not have made such an apparently heartless answer. Godwyn bowed her little heated face to hide her storm of indignation. She was not sufficiently educated even to be puzzled by this new theory of political economy, but she understood that her uncle cared more for his books than he did for the sorrows of these poor people. She had a great admiration for Mr. Bardsley generally, but could not forgive him for his indifference to the sufferings which made her grow hot all over with sympathetic anger. She had come to him with her own theory that something more ought to be done, and that the manager—Mr. Hayden—was not doing all he could, and she was determined to make her uncle interest himself about it, however much he might care for his books.

Had she grown to what are called " years of discretion" she would have known that this resolution would be difficult to carry out, for Mr. Bardsley was easy-going about all such things as ordinary sickness or sadness? From long habit he had accustomed himself to look at the phenomenon of disease with a cold curiosity which he thought was scientific. Really kind-hearted as he was, he did not feel that lively interest in his neighbours' concerns which would justify him in answering the child's anxious questions.

" I am afraid, my dear, they have brought it on themselves," he said, when she essayed to give a faint description of the miserable condition of the cottages; " it is their own mismanagement."

" But if they were taught better—if

any one—I don't know who—if any one could set them right. Mr. Hayden has no business to—he—doesn't."

He was puzzled at her incoherency, at the nervous twitch of her hands, and answered soothingly—

" Little girls shouldn't talk about what they don't understand. For my part, I have perfect confidence in Hayden. I dare say Hayden has done what he can."

" Oh, indeed he has not," she declared excitedly. " Betsy said they asked for the window to be made to open in Matty's room to let in the fresh air—oh ! uncle, it would only have cost three shillings and sixpence—and Mr. Hayden refused them. I hate Mr. Hayden !"

He looked round, much vexed, and said,

" This is all Betsy's gossip."

"Oh, indeed it is not. They told me themselves; and when poor Mrs. Meehan had a baby born she was left to die because her husband had no money to pay for food for her."

"The fellow would have had plenty if he had not spent it all at the public-house. Child," he added, in a sterner voice than he had ever used to her before, "what business have you with such histories as these?"

She did not begin to sob and cry as he had expected she would. She was too thoroughly in earnest to have time to waste in tears, and the proud little spirit, which rebelled against being found fault with, only made her the more determined to tell him all—to force him to hear the truth.

He winced as she continued, dry-eyed, with quivering lips, and eyes widely opened with pathetic, pleading looks. It was all very uncomfortable, and he began to feel as she had made him feel once or twice before—as if this little girl was somewhat too much for him. The wasted life, during which he had nursed his own private griefs, and had taken no personal interest in those of his people, leaving the widow and the fatherless to shift for themselves, was presented to him in a new and unpleasant light, and he was disagreeably startled as he looked at it.

For the first time he felt vexed and dissatisfied with Godwyn. This sort of thing, he thought, was unwholesome, and something must be done to stop it.

CHAPTER VII.

MIDSUMMER had come again. The fever was over at Dornton. A few familiar faces were missing—Matty Morrison's amongst the rest—but the roses and honeysuckles were blooming in greater profusion than usual. Humphrey was expected home for the enjoyable summer holidays, but Mr. Bardsley had taken the precaution of inviting a married sister, with her grown-up daughter, to instil proper notions of decorum into his unsophisticated charge.

Ever since that conversation about the people in the village, it had struck him that Godwyn should be a little more like other girls. It was time for her education to be commenced in good earnest, and he thought he could not have a better adviser than his sister, Mrs. Melksham, for Mrs. Melksham's own daughters were patterns of propriety. She had brought them up, as she said, " strictly," not allowing them to join too freely in the conversations of their parents, and being particularly determined that they should never argue with her, or expect her to give any reason for her orders. The nursery-gate was kept locked in Mrs. Melksham's establishment, and the school-room was judiciously apart from the rest of the household. Regular walks with the governesses, early hours, and plain diet—these were the habits in which Laura Melksham, now left a widow, had carefully trained her eldest daughter.

Dancing had been superadded, and showy instrumental music. As for the cultivation of the mind, Mrs. Melksham was really anxious about it, but she could not put her supposed superiority sufficiently on one side to be able to join freely in conversation with her daughters.

Mrs. Melksham had answered conscientiously, when her brother invited her, that she was not fond of children, but would endeavour to do her best to help him with Godwyn.

On the first morning of her arrival, she hurt the child's feelings by assuming the charge of the teapot, and dispensing the beverage with unusual care, but improved matters by proposing that Godwyn should go with her and her daughter Florry for a walk after breakfast to see the beauties of the neighbourhood.

" What has James been thinking of ?"

thought Mrs. Melksham, when Wynnie smiled and nodded repeatedly in her walk through the village. "Young ladies," she said impressively, "should not make too free with poor people."

The afternoon drive was much more disastrous, for Mr. Bardsley's *protégée* had become nervous, and, catching her foot as she dismounted from the carriage, splashed into a puddle.

"Awkward, ungainly child! we ought to do like the Roman Catholics, and send stupid and awkward girls into a convent," muttered the lady, whose silk dress had received a plentiful bespattering from the mud which had accumulated in consequence of recent rain. "There! good gracious! keep your dirty boots away from me."

Godwyn was miserable enough till the day of Humphrey's arrival. Mrs. Melk-

sham was present at the meeting, and saw
the boy dash forward, nearly knocking
the girl over with his vehement greeting;
whilst Wynnie's face lit up with the
excitement of recognition, and her little,
thin frame trembled with joy at the
sound of the voice of her playmate.

"Gently, gently!" said the matron with
a warning finger; but the children hardly
heard her, as they walked about with
merry faces, and arms locked together.
They expected, as usual, to be able to
indulge in their tumultuous pleasures.
Had not Humphrey made various sacrifices
to Godwyn's fastidious scruples, and did
he not boldly declare how he preferred
her to any of his Rugby companions?
As long ago as Easter-time the catapult
had been thrown away, because the little
girl, who so rarely shed tears, had wept

bitterly about the broken wing of a sparrow.

His favourite sports, before she came, had been hunting rats with a ferret, or squirting at the maids as he stood in ambush; but he now regarded both these amusements with a new and sublime contempt. There was no delight like making an appointment with Godwyn to look for mushrooms in the early morning, when the sun was drinking eagerly at every grass-blade and leaf dripping with dew. If, as Betsy pointed out, it was before the proper season, and there were no mushrooms to be found, there was still the excuse of looking for them, and the fun of getting up. The children had planned to spend all their days together, from these early morning hours till the time when the rippling shadows and the undulating lines lay long upon the grass, and when Mr. Bardsley was wont to descant on the "beauty of the lights."

It was too provoking that Mrs. Melksham should interfere with this programme, that she should call them punctually in to hot luncheons which they hated, because they were obliged to put on a strict decorum which turned the meals into a penance. To think that she should interfere with the greatest fun of the whole day, that of going down barefooted to the beach at low water to hunt for sea-anemones when the slippery rocks and sea-weedy places appeared !

Humphrey made a face at Aunt Laura boldly, behind her back, when she called Godwyn's attention to the state of her wet frocks, forbidding all such wild expeditions in future, and saying,

"I would not interfere with your pleasure till it was *quite* necessary."

"She means to be very kind," said
Godwyn, with pursed-up lips, and a
stolid determination not to think of
shedding a tear. But Humphrey repeated his faces again that very night,
when his aunt proposed music, and his
well-educated cousin murdered an air on
the new piano, which had been sent from
London for the occasion, by fingers pounc-
ing down on the instrument through endless variations.

"It's what they call 'Go-bang!'"
whispered the boy pertly, imitating the
dancing of the fingers over endless little
triplets, and mimicking the lightning
of the treble and the thunder of the
bass.

Godwyn's stifled laughter exploded.
And while Mr. Bardsley, a good deal

worried, tried to make an excuse for the laughter of " the pickles," Mrs. Melksham said they turned the place into a " perfect pandemonium." She gave her brother " a piece of her mind" on the subject that very night. He had wanted, as she reminded him, to have " a mother's opinion about Godwyn," and now it was useless for him to mutter that he did not wish " Nature to be supplemented by a code of morals which would put young creatures into shackles and strait-waistcoats."

It never occurred to him that any one could think the companionship between the two children whom he had adopted one of doubtful propriety, and for the first time he was alarmed for his favourite.

" It is painful and disagreeable for me to interfere, but I do it out of charity and from a real sense of duty," said the lady, seeing that she had offended her brother. "I have no doubt that that child may do well in proper hands, only she has been mismanaged. You are really very fond of her, and have never thought of the cruelty of letting her misunderstand her position in the house."

"You ought to have been a female Pope, Laura," said Mr. Bardsley, a little irritated. "Rachel never suggested that there was anything improper in the arrangement, but you have a way of speaking which suggests finality, if not infallibility."

Mrs. Melksham was offended in her turn, but thinking it better to say no more till her brother's eyes were further opened, she sailed majestically from the room, little guessing that her absence had been the excuse for the reaction to anarchy after despotism, and though it was now nearly ten o'clock at night, the children had rushed into the garden, and were parading their favourite walks, with arms locked together, the heavy·folded roses swinging into Godwyn's face, and the trumpeting of gnats resounding in her ears.

The daffodil "lights," which Mr. Bardsley would point out with the eye of an artist, had long ago melted into emerald greenness and disappeared. The cawing of the circling rooks and the overpowering melodies from the later songsters of the spring had ceased an hour before. But the change was delightful from the heat and formality of the drawing-room.

"I wish she'd go to Jericho and let us be jolly as we used to be before she came," said Humphrey, out of all patience, as his aunt's voice was heard calling authoritatively from the drawing-room,

" Godwyn ! Godwyn ! What a little Hottentot that child is ! Will somebody go and fetch her ?"

And Godwyn, with her fancy tickled irresistibly by the ridiculousness of the situation, discovered her whereabouts as before by bursting into a laugh.

*   *   *   *

The next morning Mr. Bardsley occupied the boy, determining to examine him as to his progress in Latin, but Godwyn, true to her vagrant propensities, was missing, as she often was after breakfast. Her uncle met her with a graver face than usual as she came in.

"You have been to the village?" he said, a little sternly.

She looked up in dismay, and answered,

"I have been to see Matty's mother."

"Who took you there?"

"My legs."

"That is vulgar," interposed Mrs. Melksham, who was standing near them.

"Jane was with me."

"She is too young to take care of you, and too untaught to be your associate any longer. Your aunt is right in saying that these expeditions must be stopped. Mr. Hayden met you, but you took no notice of him," said James Bardsley, looking at her reproachfully.

"Oh, then it was Mr. Hayden who made you angry with me, but it doesn't make any difference. I said long ago, when I found how cruel he was to the

Morrisons, I would never say 'Sir' to him again, and never answer his 'How are you's?' again with a smile. I'll not look at him any more. I am quite determined."

"Well, then, we must see if we can't break your determination," answered Mr. Bardsley, in a voice which she had never heard him use before. "I have already consulted with your aunt as to what must be done, and we have decided that you must stay in your own room and go without your luncheon."

He had never dreamt of punishing her before, and she tried to take this new experience with bravery and assumed indifference.

"There is nothing I should like better. I don't want to go down to luncheon. I have never liked going to luncheon since Aunt Laura has been here," the child

muttered, loud enough to be heard, looking at him for the first time with defiance
in her eyes.

" Leave *me* to manage her," said Mrs.
Melksham, when she had gone, rather
amused than otherwise by this burst of
sudden anger. " Really, James, I pity
you. I can't think what you would have
done with this little spitfire if you had
attempted to manage her any more without a woman to help you."

CHAPTER VIII.

MRS. MELKSHAM'S management of the little culprit proved to be no difficult task. Before the hour of punishment was ended Wynnie's transient flush of defiance had died out in her utter misery that her uncle should be angry with her. And though Mrs. Melksham's voice made her shrink into herself—though she flushed and her eyes fell, while the corners of her mouth were tightly compressed together—she was ready to promise anything that her guardian might require of her. It seemed rather hard in that bright Midsummer to have the discovery suddenly made that she was sadly backward in her education, and must do lessons regularly. But Aunt Laura had decided that it was necessary to break her in by a regular course of treatment. And Fate made it easier for Godwyn by letting the wonderful blaze of summer be followed by a few mild and rainy days. There was a little interval of chilliness after the languor of the heat, and it was not so hard to stay indoors whilst Humphrey wandered out to fish; though on the sudden introduction of dress-makers and lesson-books she felt like some of the characters in Humphrey's favourite stories, as if her head had been turned round in the wrong way on her shoulders, and she had reason to be in doubt as to her own identity.

The excellent fit of her new dresses,

tight, and uncomfortably stretched across the shoulders, whilst the material was buckled closely to the waist, seemed to the child—who had been hitherto allowed to have her limbs uncontrolled—faintly suggestive of a strait-waistcoat. But Uncle Bardsley approved, and said, "Ah! that's something like!" the first time his eyes lighted on the clean white dress, so that the dressmaker would have been tolerable enough without the lessons. For Godwyn who had been able to laugh when Humphrey made her brave, felt in his absence half paralysed with dread of her new aunt. A dread which resulted in stupidity and utter bewilderment; a bewilderment which only increased when she was told that she was absolutely ignorant and knew little more than a savage. Othello had been a savage, and she had rather an admiration for Othello.

But " Hottentot " conveyed more dismal associations, since one of the books she had singled out in Mr. Bardsley's library had been " Moffat's Missions in Africa," in which, like the plums in a pudding, she had picked out the stories about lions.

Mr. Bardsley believed that the child had unusual capacities. He had taught her a little Latin, and she had learnt it readily ; his own theory was that it was physical nervousness, which would wear off when she grew older, which made Godwyn seem an idiot when his sister examined her.

Flossy, who did not often have much to amuse her, laughed outright at her mother's astonishment, as the child answered to a simple historical question,

" Oh yes ! I know all about Queen

Elizabeth—she was a funny woman—she courted when she was seventy !"

"What does the girl mean ? how improper !" said Mrs. Melksham, looking in a horrified way at Flossy.

"Oh, of course," (breathlessly), " she courted Essex, you know, and then let him be put to death—all because he didn't let her know he cared for her. I *do* call that a vain thing to let a person be put to death just because he didn't send you a ring to say he cared for you."

"Is the child mad?" asked poor Mrs. Melksham hopelessly. To do her justice, she wanted to make the best out of Godwyn. But history, geography, or grammar—it was all the same, a hopeless muddle, except that which the child's imagination had seized with tenacity and as often distorted.

"She reads poetry in an unconsciously dramatic manner," said James Bardsley, a little mortified, when he was informed of this ill-success. "I think you will be really astonished if you ask her to recite Shakspeare."

But instead of being astonished, Mrs. Melksham was righteously shocked to find that the girl had committed to memory long passages of Shakspeare. Godwyn recited her best, but her auditors did not appreciate her loud apostrophising and attitudinising. A splutter of laughter came from Flossy.

"You must take those books away from her unless you wish her to go on the stage," said Mrs. Melksham to her brother. "I did not mean to speak about it in the child's presence, but now that we are alone I tell you it must be put a stop to."

James Bardsley sighed. He was frightened at the dangerous look which flashed from the child's eyes, when he told her that Mrs. Melksham said she was not again to touch any of the books of poetry in his library.

"There is evidently much that is antagonistic in their dispositions," he thought, as he noticed that something firm and almost hard seemed lately to have come into his little favourite's face, and he was scarcely surprised when a few days afterwards Mrs. Melksham came to tell him that Godwyn had disregarded her strictest prohibition and been found feasting on the forbidden books alone in her uncle's library.

Had she broken the order on purpose? It seemed difficult to say that she had, as she rushed breathlessly past her aunt, with

a scared face, up the stairs. But Godwyn
had occasional fits of defiance, which
seemed inconsistent with her usual
nervousness, and on this occasion she
had been backed up in her defiance by
indignant Humphrey, who resented this
interference with his playmate's former
habits as much as he resented her confinement over lessons in the holidays,
and long tasks of needlework.

"It comes of being a girl. A fellow
would never stand her nonsense," said
the angry boy, whose manly assumption
of contempt for any threats from his
aunt gave Godwyn's courage a fillip
which served her for a time.

"She must be made to remember this,"
so Mrs. Melksham reasoned, regretting
the alternative to which she was forced
as much as it was possible to regret
it.

"How will you make her remember it? I told her to speak to Mr. Hayden, and she still refuses to speak to him. Her will is a match for yours, in spite of any apparent nervousness; and I —I can hardly help making an idol of her, God forgive me," said Mr. Bardsley, who had an intuitive feeling that a struggle was impending between his sister and his ward, and who was also regretful now, when it was too late, that he had allowed Laura to have the arm of the law so thoroughly on her side.

He was sorry enough for his favourite, but he thought it most likely that the aunt was right. Added to this, there was his indifference of character and the inherent love of peace at all costs, which made it impossible for him to put himself in the breach.

"You leave it to *me*," said Mrs. Melksham, nodding her head. "I have never allowed myself to be thwarted by a child in my lifetime, and you may be sure that I shall not hurt her."

Mr. Bardsley was not disposed to give his countenance to any extreme form of coercion, but he felt himself getting into a mess, and did not see that anything could be done now but to leave things to take their course.

"I speak of it on the highest ground," continued the lady, "that of principle."

"Oh yes, I know," muttered James Bardsley to himself. "Lots of things that are disagreeable are done on principle."

He was uncomfortably reminded of how Rachel had objected to Godwyn's mother on principle, and was almost irritated into adding, "Please to remember that I am master here."

But after all it was he who had invited Laura to come to help him with a difficulty. It was better to settle himself to his book and to leave the women to arrange the matter for themselves, so as to gain time for reflection as to what should be done if Laura's discipline should prove to be too severe for his pet.

Mrs. Melksham's determination was made the easier from the way in which the child answered her when she caught her in her own bedroom, in which she had taken refuge in her first affright.

"You had been told not to go into the study again. How did you venture to take down the books when you had been forbidden to go?" asked. Mrs. Melksham, in the voice which Humphrey declared to be like a "cold east wind," but which had the merit of being free from the least trace of anger.

"I have always been there since I lived here. He likes to have me with him. I don't see what you have to do with it," answered the child, her little bosom heaving, with the look of defiance in her shining eyes.

It was, as James Bardsley had expected, a tussle of wills between the two, with the strength all on one side.

"You ought not to answer in that rude way," said Mrs. Melksham, looking with grave disapproval at the beauty of the flushed cheeks and the eyes shining like two stars. "I must punish you till you promise to obey my orders."

" I don't want to come down any more to-day," said Godwyn, anxious to express her contempt for such punishments.

" This room is too pretty for you while you are in your present frame of mind," said Mrs. Melksham, glancing wonderingly, as she had often glanced before, at the pink draperies and china ornaments prepared for the little alien child. " There is a very comfortable room in another part of the house, where I intend to send you. When I go to bed myself I will come and let you out. There will be a sofa there, and you can rest on it if you like. I am afraid I am too indulgent. I only require your promise that you will obey me in future to let you return to your own bedroom directly I

come to you. Betsy will take you there.
It is now four o'clock, and you will
have a good many hours for reflection
—not too many—before I come."

It was in accordance with Betsy's
entreaties that "her young lady" was to
be allowed to return to her own pretty
bedroom when the time came for sleep.
Godwyn was accustomed on the summer
nights to sit up late—too late, as Mrs.
Melksham had often declared, to be good
for her—therefore the punishment appeared at first sight a very mild one.
It was only Betsy who muttered to
herself as she coaxed the shrinking little
girl to follow her quickly to a room
in the empty wing in the older part of
the house, " It's a cruel shame to put
the weakly thing in here, when the room
ain't generally used, and she so fearsome
like."

"I don't care about it, Betsy; don't let her think that I care about it," said Godwyn, still defiant, repressing the sob which Betsy's sympathy threatened to make heave up in her little throat, and pushing away the tea and bread and butter which, contrary to orders, the old woman had provided. "Take it away; I am not hungry—I don't care to eat anything."

But when Betsy left her, her courage broke down. The kind old woman was herself partly the source of the mischief; she had told her all sorts of ghost tales of this part of the house.

There was an old piece of tapestry which Godwyn would have admired had Humphrey been with her, but which now caused little thrills of horror to run through her veins. The figures on it seemed to advance to meet her as Betsy's retreating footsteps resounded through the empty passage. Mrs. Melksham had been true to her word; she had had a sofa placed in the room, which was otherwise unfurnished. It was a comfortable sofa, and yet it seemed like irony to suppose that Godwyn could rest upon it and forget her troubles in sleep. She did not know that Mrs. Melksham's imagination was not in the least like hers, and that that lady would have had no ears for the unexplained night sounds, which, as evening drew near, made her own nerves tingle. She was stronger than she had been when Humphrey had locked her in the church—yet that had only been for a short time—the misery had soon ceased. Merciful faintness had come to her, but now she was not in the least inclined to faint. She forced herself to investigate some of the unexplained noises. The tapping, like that of bony fingers, at the small panes of glass in the window, proved to be only the branches of ivy and the stray suckers of the Virginia creeper shaken by the wind against the glass. The shuffling, which had sounded like the noise of footsteps, was, after all, only the same wind shaking the loose old tapestry. Yet the windows were terribly small and encrusted with dirt. Twilight came to that wing of the house an hour earlier than to the newer, airier rooms.

At one moment she determined to risk it, and give a sharp pull at the bell. Then she discovered that there was no bell—no means of communication with the other inmates of the house. Her nerves were at last strung to the highest possible pitch, when a horrible cry startled her ears, and there was a rush of wings near the window which curdled her blood. The ivy overhung the window, but just then she could not think of it, or remember the possible existence of any other living creature in the deserted place but herself.

Hitherto, owing to her better state of health, she had been in a wholesomer, healthier condition than during the previous winter, but now again she seemed to lose all control over her senses, and to be standing on the narrow boundary line between the seen and the un-seen.

She raised her voice as loudly as it was possible for her to raise it. The tears which she generally restrained came raining down her cheeks, and her slight frame was shaken by heaving sobs as with agony imparted by terror she

struck against the locked door till she
grazed the flesh on her little fists.

"I hate her! I hate her! Oh God!
help me not to feel so wicked," she
called aloud, as she recognised the im-
potence of her childish strength. "Why
did she shut me in here?"

"Screech as loud as you like if it's
any comfort to you, my dear. *I* am
coming," called a cheery voice from outside the window, as at the same moment
there was a clash of glass and Humphrey's round head appeared through
the crazy old frame, which he was pull-
ing to pieces.

She could see his form but not his
face, the rosiness of which was obscured
by the twilight, as he cried in a voice
of triumph—

"There! I knew the hammer would
do it in a jiffy; we shall soon have a

place big enough to lift my lady down by the ladder. Oh, you need not mind it; I determined I'd outwit her when she said she'd locked you up—and I remembered that night in the church when you were such a good little creature as never to blab. Most girls would have been blurting it out at once, but you are hardly like a girl— except in being such a coward. There —don't shake so," he added, when he clambered into the room to help her up; "*I* will take all the blame. Uncle won't be angry with *me*. Indeed, he knew all about it, though we must keep it close. I told him what I meant to do, and he actually helped me to find the ladder."

She whispered her story of the noises, and he laughed louder than ever.

" You're a queer little fish," he said in

his patronising fashion; "it's my belief the noises are all in your own fancy.

"Not that terrible scream," said Godwyn, still shrinking from the proposed descent by the ladder, trammelled as she was by the needlessly inconvenient dress which Mrs. Melksham considered to be due to the dignity of her approaching womanhood, and nineteenth century civilisation.

"Scream? Oh, to be sure, it was some rascally old owl. There's lots of ivy on that wall, and the owls are pretty abundant, I can tell you. I remember an owl was in my bedroom once—he got down the chimney—he was ruffled all over, with awful eyes. Why, if you'd been in my case we should have had an inquest the next morning," said the boy, still shaking with laughter, as he helped to lift her down.

The first serious fracas between James Bardsley and his sister took place when the former refused to blame his nephew for the daring impudence of his adventure.

"Excuse me," said Mrs. Melksham, drawing herself up, and recovering her temper as soon as her brother lost his, "but I am sure you must see now how ordinary life would soon become unbearable under such conditions as these. The girl is already perfectly unmanageable, and I decline to wait for any irreparable scene. I advise you to send her away—to some good school."

Laura, as she expressed it, "washed her hands of it" after she had given this advice as final. She and her daughter left Dornton the next morning, taking courteous leave of Mr.

Bardsley, who was a little ashamed of himself.

The upshot of this was that in a few weeks Mrs. Melksham heard from her brother, saying that he had made arrangements to send Godwyn abroad.

"I shall visit her once a year myself at Heidelberg," he wrote, to Laura's astonishment—not adding that he was so determined to free the child from the interference of his relations, and to separate her, for a time, from Humphrey, that he had broken through his solitary habits for the sake of effecting this purpose. "The English lady," he wrote, "who keeps the school, seems to be in every way an admirable person. She pays great attention to those children whose education has been neglected. The neighbourhood is beautiful—the living good. My little Godwyn will have the best instruction, both from English and foreign masters, and I shall be much disappointed if she does not return to me a good and accomplished woman."

"Who would have thought it of James?" said Mrs. Melksham, as she pondered over the letter. "Well, the child is twelve years old, and the heir to the property is fifteen. It is quite time they should be separated. Of course the property must be drained of money for the little alien's education. Well, I believe Heidelberg is as cheap as anywhere."

CHAPTER IX.

SEVEN years had passed, away and a great transformation had taken place in the manor-house at Dornton. A year before, in honour of Humphrey's coming of age, an army of white-jacketed men, imported from Exeter, had been employed, with pails and plaster, cutting out rotten patches from the damaged ceilings, renewing the wood-work and paint, and driving away the rats and owls from the older and previously uninhabitable part of the house.

There were a few things about which

Mr. Bardsley had been arbitrary. No workmen had been allowed to interfere with the old remains of Elizabethan architecture, of which he was justly proud; but there were other matters in which Humphrey and the innovators had been allowed to have their way. Close to the old terrace a lawn had been clipped for Badminton, crôquet being abandoned as a middle-class amusement, and the newer fashioned tennis not yet introduced; whilst a domed conservatory had been built at the end of the drawing-room, which lightened it considerably, and glorified it with flowers.

Mr. Bardsley sighed a little over these supposed improvements, which had resulted, as he acknowledged, from his determination to send Humphrey to Oxford. From that time the younger man had had the upper hand over the elder one, and—though Mr. Bardsley was still accustomed to command respect in all particulars, and to be as insistant as ever about trifles—he found himself compelled to admit Humphrey's friends, and, with them, his own relations, to his house, making a grace of the necessity, and, whenever it was not possible for him to hide himself in his own sanctum, forcing himself to be punctiliously polite to his visitors, in spite of his openly-acknowledged objection to company.

It was July, and Humphrey had just completed his term of absence at the University. The colours were as brilliant at Dornton as they had been at Midsummer seven years before. The sky was as blue as turquoise, with floating clouds; the liquid sapphire of the sea was again shot with green, like—as the children used to say—to a peacock's feathers, and the cliffs were bright with patches of lingering gorse. But the young man was still somewhat discontented with his retreat, and had a vague sense of something wanting in it, which made it contrast unfavourably with the grass-plot in the college court, where, but a short time since, the lime trees had been musical with bird and bee. His college friends were dispersed on walking tours, reading parties, and boating excursions, through some of the most beautiful scenery in the British islands and the continent of Europe. But Humphrey had already, in the long vacations, visited the Highlands, the mountains of Wales, Keswick, and Grasmere. He had been to Cowes and Scarborough, Switzerland, and the Rhine, the Pyrenees and the Apennines, and his uncle could not be thought unreasonable in hoping that he would settle down for a time amongst the lanes and streams of one of the most picturesque, if retired, watering places in Devonshire.

The old man was naturally proud of his heir. For Humphrey had grown up to be as strong as a young Hercules, and handsome enough for a modern, if not for an ancient, Apollo. It was difficult to see what purpose had been accomplished by Humphrey's stay at Oxford, except that, as Mr. Bardsley said, the boy had learnt to be a gentleman. Humphrey had imbibed some sentiment from his early friendship with Godwyn, and the combination of beauties for which Oxford is probably unrivalled, as a scene of mingled sweetness and solemnity, seemed to have fired his

imagination. He was never tired of
descanting on the cool gardens and grey
cloisters, the meadows and venerable
structures, girded round by the waters
of the Isis and the Cherwell. He could
talk about the solitude and beauty of
the Magdalen and Christ Church walks, but
he admitted that he had been glad enough
to escape to them from the routine of
lectures and daily trammels of ordinary
college life.

Humphrey was wont to say, without
being in the least ashamed of it, that he
had done as little as it was possible for
a man to do at Oxford. He could
play a few tunes on the violin, and—
dabbling a little in water-colours—had
found subjects enough to stock his port-
folios in the woods and straggling
villages, with glimpses of the broad river
towards Thame in one direction, and

Farringdon in another. The wonder was,
that putting on the steam at the last,
with the aid of an experienced "coach,"
he had managed to scrape through his
examinations. A more languid fellow,
except in the cricketing and rowing, and
the dabbling in art, in which he thought
he excelled, it would have been difficult
to find in that July weather in all the
county of Devonshire.

He was indolent but never ill-tempered;
no one had any fault to find with him,
except of the negative kind. He was
sometimes tempted in his own secret
heart to doubt if his ample leisure was
quite a gain to him. But there was
never any business to be done—his uncle
always managed to do without him—
and there was generally time to be killed.
He knew that he was unusually popular with the majority, and never troubled

himself to inquire into the verdict which never reached him of the more cynical minority. Most people thought that the younger Mr. Bardsley was charming— never priggish or dictatorial, which was considered to be the more surprising as he was the heir to so large a property, and as certain deposits, left from the reading which had filtered through his mind, enabled him to talk well on a good many subjects. Did he not content himself with the simple pleasures of the country in such a dead time of the year, when many of his friends were in London?

" He is perfectly harmless, without any vicious tastes, and that is the best you can say for him," decided Mrs. Melksham in her usual incisive manner, when Rachel declared that their nephew was altered for the better.

As to the paper-mills, by which the money that was to be his in the future was realised, it never occurred to Humphrey to trouble himself at all about them. He had been accustomed to leave the workpeople entirely to Mr. Hayden, understanding from his uncle that " the less Hayden was interfered with the better."

For the *verve* and brightness of his boyhood, for the affluence of youthful spirits, which had at one time distinguished him, the heir was no longer remarkable. A fastidious critic might have deplored that idleness and supineness should be allowed to sap the foundations of such a character; those who loved him might have guessed that Humphrey had still his generous impulses, his reserves of unexpected strength. At present he was supposed to be much smitten by the attractions of a pretty and rather fast brunette, who, with her mother, was staying at Dornton. There was not, as Mrs. Melksham remarked, "a more spoiled child in all Devonshire than Olive Neale," whose mother, a bright matron of some fifty-five years, in rather weak health, was entirely managed by her.

Whether Humphrey was really "smitten" by the charms of Olive Neale was a fact best known to himself. It argued little that he did not take the pains to deny the imputation. If they had said that Humphrey was about to commit a murder, he probably would not have troubled himself to deny it. He was certainly artist enough to be impressed by the beauty of the girl, brilliant with a brilliancy of colouring which scarcely ever survives childhood.

Mrs. Melksham, as she confided to her

sister, " had her eye on Olive." For she was also a visitor at Dornton—not with her elder daughter, Florence, who had satisfied her mother's expectations by marrying a man who was not only rich, but had also been knighted—but with a second daughter who was barely seventeen, and whom Humphrey would compare to Göthe's Gretchen, with her fair hair falling round her shoulders.

Olive Neale looked upon Christine Melksham as a pretty foil to herself, for the child was so far from being a rival to her, that whilst her pale face contrasted artistically with Olive's bright cheeks and flashing eyes, Christine was timid and nervous, needing protection and help. The two girls " grouped," as Humphrey with his artistic slang declared, but Olive had all the talk to herself. All the youthful vigour seemed to be subdued in Christine; she was overawed and constantly depressed, especially in her mother's presence.

All children are not so easily moulded as some parents think, and Mrs. Melksham was constantly deploring that it was not *her* fault if, in Christine's case, her usual system fell short. She really loved Christine as much as she had loved Florence, and was even now planning excursions and picnics to try to rouse her out of her melancholy. But if she could have seen the gleam of hostility which occasionally flashed from her child's eyes, she would have been sorry for her. For the poor girl, who was neither stupid nor indolent, but who had been crammed against her will with useless accomplishments, was for ever having it dinned into her ears how fortunate her sister had been to make so good a match,

and that she must also marry well, for
the benefit of her family, that she should
not stand in the way of her younger
sister and a younger brother, who cost
so much in their education at their
respective schools, and in wearing out
their clothing. And Mrs. Melksham would
have recognised her mistake in thinking
that all her girls had been sent into the
world simply to conform to her will and to
minister to her pleasure, could she have
guessed how her daughter's refinement was
outraged by these worldly ideas. Christine,
she justified herself by saying, required
" rousing ;" she never would have talked
so had it been Florence. Some girls, she
would declare, were too forward, and
required keeping back, but in this case
the danger lay in the other direction.

"Poor   Aunt   Laura !"   Humphrey
laughed at her for the stiffness which he

said was "moral rheumatism." She wanted to have her child perfectly trained, and to look back upon her work with self-approval when it was ended, as a thing rounded and completed like a properly-proved sum. She could admit of no flaws or imperfections in her work, and that the girl should obey her for her own good, and know no opinions but her own, would have been like a strain of music in her ears. But that her daughter should show an independent will; that she should prefer to stay at home when it was good for her health to go out; that she should hate music, though money had been wasted on teaching it to her, and that absolute neglect should be preferable to anything like despotic severity—all this was incredible. In Christine's case it had ended in a melancholy distaste for everything—

a distaste which was not incompatible
with a little liking for admiration, but
which only made Dornton tolerable to
her because it was better to be there
than with the noisy little companions who
dinned her in the holidays at her uncon-
genial home.

What distress of mind the poor girl
would have suffered if she could have
known the secret explanation of their
long stay at Dornton, and the humiliating
fact that her mother had that " eye " of
which she was always boasting on Humphrey as well as Olive, for certain
schemes of her own, I am saved from
recording. But Mr. Bardsley was
sharper than she was. Though he
had grown more grey and wrinkled,
and more spare, though he occasionally
condescended to the help of a stick, to
enable him to walk as erect as ever,

and though he was secluded constantly in the privacy of his own room, yet his faculties were still remarkably keen; he saw through the ladies' plans, and he too had a favourite scheme. He was conscious of nervousness in endeavouring slightly to hint at his intentions for the future to his sister Rachel on the eve of the day when, after seven years' absence, his favourite, Godwyn Payton, was expected to arrive, carefully chaperoned, to take up her residence in the home which for the present was to be hers.

After her first remonstrance against receiving Ellen's child, he remembered that Rachel had never been guilty of interference. It was easier to speak to Rachel than it would have been to speak to Laura, now that the infirmities of advancing years reminded him that death might some day take him by surprise.

"I have not seen Godwyn," he said with trembling voice, "for two whole years. You know I have not been sufficiently strong lately to travel as far as Heidelberg. She seemed so happy when I last saw her, dear child, leaping about like a young fawn as she insisted on guiding me herself about the old ruins, quoting as she used to quote—how they laughed at her for quoting Shakspeare! —passages from Longfellow's 'Hyperion,' illustrative of her favourite places— quoting, aye, and translating, bits from her favourite German poets. How surprised Laura will be when she sees her, and hears her talk! and how glad I am I did not send her to one of those dreadfully mismanaged schools which one sometimes hears of—schools which send out their supply of mothers for a future generation, with a black ewe or two to blacken the wool of the innocent young lambs!"

"You cannot be sure how your experiment will have turned out, James; it was an experiment, to say the least of it," said Rachel, hesitatingly. "Laura" —and he guessed from her intonation that she thought the sentiment an unkind one—"Laura thinks you may have to part with her again if she should prove headstrong."

"Laura *thinks!*" he said, starting up angrily, and repeating the words contemptuously. "I will not have any more of Laura's meddling in my concerns; I tell you it was Laura's fault I have been deprived of her all this time. I hear golden opinions from Heidelberg, but I cannot tell you how much I miss her—the darling child! I could not be robbed twice of her for any consideration on earth."

"You seem to know her well; has she always written to you?"

"Always. Yes, she has been such a faithful correspondent, and all her little heart as clear to me as white paper."

"How about the father?" asked Rachel, with a feeling as if she were treading on eggs, speaking doubtfully and dropping her voice. "I remember your telling me a dreadfully long story about him years ago. Is this story to be hidden from the daughter still? I have no very distinct idea about it."

There was a pause, and then he said,

"Let her rest in ignorance. It is no sin to be glad I have not heard from him, surely."

"If you think it is right to keep her in ignorance—you know your own con-

cerns best—but I should have thought,"
commenced the lady doubtfully, and then
suddenly stopped, remembering it was to
her own interest to keep on good terms
with James.

James had been good to her all these
years. He had not only supplied
her with the necessaries but with the
superfluities of life, and the fingers were
covered with rings which Rachel extended,
instead of further words, with a sort of
flourish, as if to dismiss a subject on
which she had become fearful of ex-
pressing too strong an opinion. The new
element of dissipation which had been
introduced into the quiet household at
Dornton, the picnics, rides, and drives
which were constantly being planned by
Mrs. Melksham, Humphrey, or Mrs.
Neale, were as distasteful to Rachel as
they were to her brother. Olive Neale

had been occasionally scornful to the quiet lady, who in her turn had been thoroughly disgusted by the manners which she considered to be " unmaidenly" and loud. Altogether the new generation had become a perplexing puzzle to Rachel, but her heart had turned by way of relief to the absent Godwyn.

"Speak out, Rachel," said her brother, who did not wish to consider the subject dismissed.

" I am thinking about by-and-by."

" *I* often think of it."

"Humphrey is the heir; you have already promised him your fortune, and you—you are not a man to go back from your promise."

" No, you have hit it. I also adopted this dear child, but I cannot give her what I had already promised to Humphrey; and I—I have uncomfortable thoughts about it sometimes myself. I don't want to be contriving, after I have educated her, how to take my change out in my own increased happiness; it is of the girl as well as of Humphrey that I want to think. I don't want to be such an old fool as to wish to turn her into a plaything."

"Well, then, if you can't be sure that she will always live in such luxurious circumstances, why not let her have something else satisfactory to fall back upon?"

"I have given her that already in the best education it was possible for me to give her," he answered, thinking his logic irrefragable.

"Why not let her have practice in teaching?"

"I cannot bear to think of it."

"But it may be necessary to think of it."

"I hope not. Do you remember how fond Humphrey used to be of her?"

"When they were mere children."

"But he may be fond of her *now*," persisted the old man. "If Humphrey marries to please me, he will marry the child of my adoption."

Rachel shook her head.

"He will do nothing of the kind, especially if you try to press him on the subject. He will marry Olive Neale."

"Heaven forbid!" said James a little warmly. "I shall exercise no open pressure, of course, but I have my own opinion on the subject; and I thought," he continued nervously, "I would just give you a gentle hint, Rachel. Women have a way sometimes of influencing—I am anxious about it."

Rachel shook her head. Her experience of life had taught her to discourage all such schemes, but her brother seemed to be caught on the horns of a strange dilemma, and his device seemed to him to be his best way out of it. She sincerely pitied him.

CHAPTER X.

IN spite of Rachel's warnings it was difficult for Mr. Bardsley to help being inconveniently, and, as Humphrey thought, almost disagreeably, glad on the morning of Godwyn's expected arrival. Forgetful of all his good resolutions he gave pointed hints, so that the young man's memory went back to an episode of his boyhood almost with an emotion of anger and regret.

"What a fool he must have made himself about that babyish girl, that every one should be able to laugh at him about it to his face! and what a confounded nuisance it would be if people should form all sorts of theories on the strength of his 'calfishness!'"

He felt, in his first scorn at the allusions made by his uncle, as if it would be necessary for him to come to an immediate understanding about the matter, and to make Mr. Bardsley then and there acquainted with the fact that Godwyn's coming home was a subject of perfect indifference to him. And yet in his heart of hearts he could not deny that he had a sort of anxiety to see her again; he had sometimes thought it was the anxiety which made him feel unsettled.

It was well for Godwyn—whose lady friend parted with her in London early that morning, after seeing her safely into a first-class carriage, to make her way to

Devonshire for the first time alone—that she knew nothing of the little scheme which might prove so fatal to her happiness. The weather was fine and clear, and she had had a good view of the surrounding prospect, which brought back strange remembrances, before Mr. Bardsley came to meet her at the neighbouring station. The old man was less reticent than usual in his unwonted excitement. The effort had evidently been a great one for him, and to Godwyn—to whom it seemed quite odd to be treated with the deference due to a grown-up young lady —this unnecessary fuss about her comforts was vexatious rather than pleasing.

"Is that quite the thing? I don't understand much about costumes, but wouldn't it have been better if you had put on a less schoolgirlish dress, my dear?" said Mr. Bardsley, when the carriage-wheels were moving slowly over the road, and his ward, after being warmly entreated to rest herself on the cushions, was sitting by his side with her hand in his. The dress which she wore was of some coarse and cheap material, none the fresher for her journey, and he noticed with some annoyance that the pale neutral tint was trying to a complexion in which a red glow, caused by exposure to wind and sun, had replaced the usual fair, cool pink.

"It is my travelling dress—one of my school-dresses, you know. I am only a schoolgirl, and you did not write to me to put on any better," she answered, perceiving his annoyance, in the low, sonorous tones which had usually proved effectual in soothing his vexation.

"Ah! you have no idea how smart we

have all grown at Dornton; times have
changed since you were with us," he said
with a slight laugh, not liking to confess
to her what reason he had to fear that
an ungainly appearance would put her in
the wrong at once with some of his guests
at the manor-house.

Quick-sighted Godwyn understood
more than he explained to her. But
she did not tell him that she understood.
And when they reached the well-remem-
bered height leading to the manor-house
and commanding an extensive panorama,
after a toilsome ascent up a winding
road at the back of the cliff, the sight
quickly obliterated all thoughts of self.
Her astonishment at the transformation
which the house and grounds had under-
gone was only equalled by her surprise,
when she was ushered into the drawing-
room. She had not been prepared

for the appearance of a girl apparently a few years older than herself, *piquante*, black-eyed, brown-skinned, carmine-cheeked, and elegantly got up, with the white folds of her alpaca dress falling in lines of drapery which showed the supple grace of her figure, who advanced to meet her, and introduced herself, speaking in a manufactured sort of voice, probably, as Godwyn thought, founded on somebody else's way of speaking.

"Mrs. Melksham is dressing for dinner," she said. "You are later than we thought you would be. Christine and I dressed earlier to be ready in case you should be late. I am under the uncomfortable necessity of introducing myself—your intended friend, Olive Neale. This is your cousin—Christine Melksham."

Even in the assumed gravity of Olive's

speech there was a little sarcastic lingering on the word "cousin," as another
girl, pale and shrinking, with her fair
hair in two long plaits, and a black velvet
bodice—recalling to Godwyn's mind, as
to Humphrey's, the likeness to Göthe's
Gretchen—followed her from the conservatory, in which both of them had
been sitting. The conservatory, was
one of the surprises—lighting up the
old-fashioned drawing-room, which had
formerly been so dark—with its tesselated
pavement, its baskets of trailing creepers,
and its sweet-scented flowers and evergreens.

But the greatest surprise of all was
when a third person, dressed as a
cricketer—also in "virgin white" a little
mud-bespattered in places, as it contrasted with Olive Neale's alpaca, and
with a coppery shining on his cheeks

and nose, showing that he too had been exposed during the last few days to the scorching brightness of the weather—stepped from beneath the flowering clematis to the inlaid polished floor of the drawing-room, just as she felt her face growing redder and redder in its bashfulness, and held out his hand.

Could this be Humphrey?—this fine tall fellow, so like a regular athlete? He must, she thought, be six feet high, for Godwyn was much over five feet herself, and yet she had to look up to him. The face, she thought, contrasted rather oddly with the clean-limbed figure. To *her* mind the features were by no means those of the Apollo type; the eyes were too dreamy, the expression too languid, for a man.

She was forced to look up to him as

she answered Olive's greeting, and as she did so she noticed something which disturbed her. The languid expression of the face passed away for a moment, and she fancied she saw surprise, almost disappointment, in the gaze which he fixed upon her.

She dropped his hand, and the redness which Mr. Bardsley had deplored, changed suddenly into rivers of scarlet, overflowing her face and neck. Olive lifted her eyebrows. The " mind you fall in love with her" manner in which Mr. Bardsley had spoken to Humphrey that morning was too fresh in his memory to make him kind to her at that moment; and the warm, honest affection of boyhood which seven years ago he had lived through, and done with, seemed to him now a thing dead and ridiculous as he looked at Olive and pronounced her the prettier of the two. Yet the chivalry in him forced him to pay a compliment to the friend of his childhood as soon as she was out of hearing, and when Mr. Bardsley himself, seeing her confusion, had insisted on showing her the way to her room.

"It is a varying face, just as it used to be, but the expression is more earnest and thoughtful," he said. "You don't see her to advantage after she has been travelling; it is few persons who can travel as if they were wrapped in cotton wool."

"What a long speech!" laughed Olive, stung by the unusual praise of another. "It reminds me of the sentimental tales Miss Bardsley has told me. Did you ever hear, Christine, of a big boy who used to walk about carrying his little 'cousin,' as he called her, on his back over streams which were too deep to wade, and slippery rocks? One day a painter met the innocents loaded with wild flowers, and asked to be allowed to take a sketch of them. They remind me, those two, of Paul and Virginia."

Humphrey was like most young men, unable to bear this sort of banter. On the spur of the moment he answered,

"I remember another Arcadian story of a little girl who was led about like a sort of pet lamb by an oldish man who doted on her, and a boy who was more like a rollicking calf; what a sensation he used to make by breaking down the fences!"

Olive laughed.

"There are fences still."

"Yes, but I doubt if I have enough energy left to break them down."

"It is of no use for you to pretend; you used to admire her very much *then*."

"I was a boy of fifteen, and she a girl of twelve," he said, with a touch of irritability at her continued raillery.

"A babyish girl for her age?" asked Olive, with her roguishly rallying look, and he was ashamed of himself that he did not answer, but hurried away also to prepare for dinner.

Meanwhile Mr. Bardsley was conducting his ward through the hall—in which she used to frighten herself as a child by fancying skeleton heads in the suits of armour—now decorated with statuary and Minton's tiles. They passed by the "Night and Morning," "Eurydice," and "Diana," with a large hall fireplace with tiles grotesquely wrought in blue and white, and ascended a handsome flight of stairs leading to another part of the house.

"Do you remember it?" asked Mr.
Bardsley as she halted, recognising the
fact that they were in the old wing which
she had hated seven years before for its
barrenness and ghastliness, but which
was now brightened up and divided into
bed-rooms. "We call it the 'Maiden's
Wing.' Olive's room is close to yours—
Christine's underneath."

The old Elizabethan windows had been
kept unaltered, and the room had been
furnished in keeping with high-backed
chairs, oval mirrors, and neutral-tinted
curtains. No bright colours had been
allowed except on the dressing-table;
there old Betsy had been allowed to
indulge her foible. It was the same
table, with its little knickknacks, which
Godwyn had used in her childhood.

"She *would* have her own way there,"
said Mr. Bardsley, lingering. "Betsy

will get you anything you want; she will see to the unpacking of the box."

"You won't find a speck of dust, Miss, not if you was to try," said the faithful old housekeeper, lingering as she came to wait upon her. "What a sight it is to see your bonny face again!"

"I am glad you have given me the dear old dressing-table, Betsy," said Godwyn, looking at the piece of Flemish point which she so well remembered, fastened round the toilet-table, and got up by skilful fingers, with the muslin top and pink ribbons which she had thought so pretty in her childhood.

"Does it come natural to you, Miss?"

"Oh yes, perfectly; it is like a dream coming back again—a very pleasant dream."

The loud whirring of the gong for dinner startled her, just as, with the old woman's assistance, she had managed to take off the travelling costume which had been trodden upon by dirty boots in the steamer, and soiled by dust in the railway journeys, and to put on another school-girlish dress, at which the old woman looked in dissatisfied silence.

Betsy's look was wasted on her, but she declared she was not hungry, with a new sort of nervousness about going down, and felt, as she entered the drawing-room, just as she had felt when she was a child, as if Mrs. Melksham's greeting was not thoroughly cordial, and as if there was something in the presence of this lady which jarred upon what was most sensitive in her organization.

She noticed that Olive's manner seemed to be a little mocking and disdainful—that she remarked something in an aside with a tittering laugh, and that Christine looked round in a fright and said "'Sh!" Again she wished that she were not a woman, and did not possess that fatal facility of blushing. What could they mean? Were they making themselves merry at the cheapness of her dress? The shaft—whatever it might have been—sped harmless directly that very probable explanation occurred to her.

She could control the first impulse which prompted her to start back like a touched sensitive plant, and it might have been Olive's turn to shrink from the direct open honesty of her eyes. But again face, throat, and ears shared the crimson glow. She was thankful to the hothouse flowers, mixed with ferns and grasses, in aërial crystal vases, and to the candelabra containing wax candles, standing daintily amidst china Cupids, holding baskets of sweetmeats, which hid her from Humphrey as she took her place at the dinner-table.

And he who had thought so much of her in her absence, that he had secretly been annoyed with himself for attaching a mysterious importance to this absent girl's power over him of which he could not despoil her, now found it tolerably easy to forget that she was present.

Godwyn could just see that he was engrossed with Olive, with whom he carried on a conversation in so low a voice that it could not be overheard by the other guests at the dinner-table. An

Oxford friend of Humphrey's sat next to her, but she answered all his questions rather vaguely in monosyllables.

She had told Betsy that this home-coming was like a pleasant dream, and she had felt so till within the last few hours, but now it was like waking dis-agreeably out of sleep.

" Tired with your journey, dear ?" asked Mr. Bardsley across the table.

The question recalled her to the fact that she was treating the Oxford friend badly. She exerted herself to talk to him—exerted herself still when the ladies returned into the drawing-room. Olive's quizzing was continued so openly that she could not but be aware of it, but Aunt Rachel came and sat by her, morally throwing her mantle over her, till the two young men sauntered in, having left Mr. Bardsley to his usual retirement.

Then it appeared that Humphrey's "all right" was quite sufficient to decide on the rival merits of piquet or écarté, just as it sanctioned in the daytime the playing of cricket, lawn tennis, picnicking or boating parties. His trouble seemed to be to kill time, and after extending his long length wearily on the sofa, while Olive amused him with some of those fireworks on the piano at which Godwyn could not help remembering he had laughed when he was a boy, he settled himself, as she supposed, to cards for the evening.

After a suggestion from Aunt Rachel that as Godwyn did not play piquet or whist she should take her turn at the piano—a suggestion quickly negatived by Mrs. Melksham, who remembered that the music was not unpacked, and that her so-called " niece" must be tired with her journey—the opportunity occurred for which the girl had been longing all the evening, and she escaped, undisturbed, into the silence of the garden.

A silver cloud hung like a diaphanous veil over the moon's shining face. The various influences which had acted on her throughout the exciting day, and the divine beauty of the evening, affected her in a way which was altogether unusual. She felt somehow like a beggar at the gates of Paradise, exiled outside the shining gates, and only catching the distant echoes of the heavenly harmonies.

She sat silent and depressed on one of the garden seats, closing her eyes, how long she knew not, till a big tear detached itself from her eyelashes and rolled slowly down her cheeks, recalling her to consciousness, only just in time, for there were footsteps approaching her,

and, looking up, she saw the sheen of
Olive's white dress and heard Humphrey's
steps on the gravel as he flung a bouquet
into her lap.

" It is too late for your favourite cycla-
mens, but I brought the best I could get.
You used to be fond of orchids," he said
with a forced laugh; " they are all gone
too, but I have brought you roses and
forget-me-nots."

He noticed in the moonlight the des-
pondent droop of the mouth, the glossy
lustre and crispness of the hair, and his
conscience reproached him in a way for
which it was difficult to account, for the
long heavy sigh which had just escaped
her. Was this home-coming a disappointment, and if it was could he help it?
Nothing could bring back the happy sim-
plicity of childhood again. Mrs. Melksham, by her enforced separation, had

shown her wisdom by placing the barrier of years between them, and nothing short of a miracle could bridge it over.

" You are as romantic as a poetess— you believe in moonlight. The moon, my dear, is out of fashion," chimed in Olive's voice.

" Miss Neale's friends are in London at this season of the year, and no doubt she grudges them their whirl of excitement," added Humphrey a little spitefully, so vexed was he with his new friend at that moment.

" We missed you over our cards, and this kind coz of yours was so anxious about you, that nothing would suit him but we must both of us come and look for you forthwith. What on earth tempted you here? Did you come in search of the birds that have tired themselves out, and have only twitters left for the autumn days? Nightingales don't sing now."

"Ah! you have heard of my escapades as a spoiled child," answered Godwyn, without the least touch of offence in the voice which was so sonorous and melodious that it was apt to sound like a sweet strain of music in Mr. Bardsley's ears, and struck even Olive Neale with something like surprise. "My foolishness gives you something to laugh at—I hope you consider it my redeeming point—I have a keen sense of the ridiculous myself; it has always done me good."

It was the first long speech she had made at all, and, after all, Olive thanked her for giving a cheerful turn to the conversation; it was better than making it solemn and dramatic.

Only the old man guessed that there

was something amiss as she went to bid him " good night" in his own apartment, and he, holding her at arm's length, asked,

" What is the matter with my little girl ?"

She laughed it off in his presence, and even he could never have guessed how she inconsistently and apparently without reason sobbed herself to sleep that night, thinking of her mother's grave far away in India—fancying, too, as she sometimes fancied, that her mother's spirit was near her, watching over her to comfort her, and wondering, if her father were not dead, why he should continue to neglect her.

CHAPTER XI.

GODWYN woke early the next morning, before any other member of
the household was stirring. She looked
out of her picturesque window—beneath
which a few blocks of old stone carv-
ing, which had been discovered when
the workmen renovated the building,
were strewn in picturesque confusion—
and tried to flatter herself that it reminded her of the ruins at Heidelberg,
plumed with fern and foxglove, in which
she had delighted. There was a scent
of sweet-briar, whilst the sun, which

had not long emerged from its eastern gates of pearl, chasing away the ebon-haired night, was drinking the drops of dew from the closely-shaven grass. And there was the old lawn, where she had heard the wood-dove's coo, where songs had burst in springtime from hundreds of little joyous throats, where the speckled-breasted thrushes used to be so busy amongst the flowers, and where the bold robin was wont to come in winter, to be fed by her breadcrumbs.

She sighed. It came back to her like a day of childhood. But she was young, and at the age when regrets cannot last. And though it was still like the awakening from a dream, and she remembered that the awakening had not been yesterday what she expected, yet she liked to revive the pleasant associations connected with the place. In an hour or two she knew that the delightful sensations of quiet and rest about the house would be dispelled by noise and glitter. But now she had it for a short time all to herself.

She could creep noiselessly through the decorated drawing-room, newly brightened with French looking-glasses, in which she remembered the ebony tables and faded Turkey carpet, to a flight of steps which led straight into the garden. Most of the garden had been altered, but there was still one part of it left untouched, where the sweet-williams, tall white lilies with golden centres, blue larkspurs, and striped carnations grew almost without cultivation, making a pleasing variety from the blazing sameness of scentless bedding plants.

Here Godwyn for a while could dream on "all the things that had been," breathing the cool freshness of the air, and blaming herself for the unrest, the fear, and the foreboding with which the clear shining morning seemed to be out of keeping. After breakfast she had determined to face the realities of her new life, and to try to get her uncle to explain to her some of the things which puzzled her. "Uncle" she called him, lingering affectionately on the word, though she had begun to doubt its literal application to herself. Uncles might not be much to some people, but in her case the term included father and mother, sister, brother— everything that was charming and attractive. Till yesterday she had looked upon Humphrey as a brother, but she felt that something had come to change the simple liking he had had for her.

"There is a mystery somewhere, which I *must* try to fathom," she said sturdily to herself, as she sought Mr. Bardsley in his sanctum. He, too, had been up early, and had slept lightly that night. His hand shook as she knocked at the door, and he hastily replaced a portrait, which he had taken from its morocco case, where it had lain hidden till lately when it had ceased to sting him with sharp memories. It was an exquisite picture of Godwyn's mother, in the very prime of her beauty.

"I am not quite certain," he said doubtfully to himself, when the girl entered the room, "but I think her mother was the prettier—yet the child's face is wonderfully expressive."

There was the same tall, lithe figure,

the same nut-brown hair, chestnut only at the temples, and the same deep thoughtful eyes. But Ellen's eyes had been grey-green, suiting the brown hair like the colour of a young hind; Godwyn's were hazel, like the soft dark eyes of the roe, with long lashes on the eyelids. Ellen had had the colour of a rose, but Godwyn's complexion—now that the redness of travel had passed off—was rather pale; there was too much strength, perhaps, in the breadth of the brow, and the mouth was a trifle too large and flexible to entitle her, as Nellie Payton had been entitled, to the verdict of absolute beauty.

"All the better," thought the old man, remembering Nellie Payton's history, and studying his darling with stolen glances, though—hypocrite as he was—he pretended to be deeply engaged with an abstruse book, which looked to the girl, as she stepped up to him, to be dry as dust and ashes. He did not notice her till she placed her hand gently on his arm, and spoke as if she feared to disturb the silence.

" Will you let me be your secretary? or teach me to read aloud to you? It is not possible for me to lead an idle life, but there is nothing I should like better than waiting upon *you*. You know—if the truth is told me—I ought to earn my own livelihood. Send me away from Dornton, if you think it would be better. If not, cannot I be trained to lighten your labours ?"

" My labours, as you call them, are of no use to anyone," he said, startled by her request, and gazing with some alarm at the strained, wistful look which had suddenly appeared in the face he rightly called "expressive." "Child, who has been meddling with you? It is your duty to enjoy yourself. Live like the flowers and the butterflies; you have nothing to do with new-fangled notions about gaining your own livelihood."

"Fraulein Leibrecht did not call them 'new-fangled.' I talked about them to her."

"I always thought Fraulein Leibrecht a very sensible woman, but it was not sensible to venture to interfere between us," he said, a little angrily. And then, relenting—"I heard how wonderfully steady and clever you had become at school. She dressed you up in all the virtues."

"She liked to believe good of me," said the girl, very softly. "You know

I lost my mother when I was such a little child. Fraulein was like a mother to me. She never interfered with or contradicted me more than she was quite obliged."

"And no one," he interrupted, "shall contradict you here. You are mistress of this house, child. I was very fond of your mother."

She did not notice the intonation with which he dwelt on the last words, but continued,

"She was not like a schoolmistress. Words can hardly tell how I enjoyed my life with her, for I had no home-friend, no confidante. But that must all go now. I lose my place in the old life in which I was active and oc-cupied every hour in the day, and if you want me to be happy you must give me plenty to do here."

" You will have cousins here."

" Are they *really* my cousins ?"

" Never mind, my dear—you and Christine must be like sisters; I do not care what name you give the relationship."

" But if they are rich, and I am poor—if I must go away some day— is it wise to put me in the position of mistress of this house? Will it not create a feeling against me. Let me take a lower place, and then no one will dislike me. I came to you at the very outset that you might grant me my request."

She was sitting at his feet now, and looking pleadingly up to him.

She astonished him considerably by speaking about things as if she were fifty years old. He began to think rightly that his " little girl" would never come back to him any more.

His own way had been comfortably to get rid of difficulties by quietly ignoring them, and he began to see that this independent will might cause him some perplexity.

"Do not talk in this way before your aunts," he said.

She did not answer, but she looked at him with worlds of meaning in those widely-opened, gazelle-like hazel eyes of hers which seemed to read people, when she chose it, uncomfortably through and through. She waited, it seemed, and meditated. It was the first hint that direct straightforwardness would not answer in this new circle to which she had been introduced.

"Must I not ask them *about my father?*" she said presently. "I have been thinking and trying to recollect.

I never saw much of him—I used to be so much with my mother. But where my father is, there, perhaps, I ought to go."

"Not if he does not want you," he answered sharply.

He was driven into the answer without intending it to be cruel. But as he saw the quiver of the tremulous mouth, the sudden shrinking as if some sharp instrument had inflicted a wound which she was determined to bear, he was indignant with himself for his irritability.

"My dear," he said, "*why* will you torture me with these unnecessary questions? If I don't answer you, it is because it is good for you that I should be silent. Have I not always been a father to you, ready to spoil you?"

And as she crept closer to him,
forced to be content with his answer,
he tried to comfort himself for deceiving her with the reflection that if the
evil which had happened to her father
was great, and if it had driven him to
desperation, it was at least unknown to
her whose happiness might be threatened
by it. Had not her mother wished to
shield her from it?

"I must forgive you for having mysti-
fied me," said the girl, looking up
brightly, after an inward struggle in
which the eager throb of anxiety was
subdued by the habit of dependence.
"I must trust you when you have been
so good to me. Life would be nothing
to us without trust. But I wish you
could have told me a little more about my
father."

"Then we are to have no more of

these uncomfortable conversations, and you must seal the contract with a kiss," he answered, ignoring the pleading tone of her last sentence.

There was no resisting him. He still lived a partially retired life, but since Godwyn had been sent to him he was far less eccentric. A pleasant, unaffected old man she thought him, struggling against the attacks and weaknesses of the first stage of old age, but making no secret of the struggle.

She did not wonder that she had almost worshipped him when she had been a child, and would rather have remained with him, had she been allowed to do so, than have joined Olive and Christine in a walk on the cliffs.

In the evening there was the same luxurious dinner, with the introduction of " a little music " after it, to which

Godwyn was again asked to contribute her quota, Mrs. Melksham again suggesting that as she could barely have had time to unpack her boxes it was hardly fair to include her in the programme.

"The box containing my music was lost in the coach; they say it will come tomorrow, but it has not come yet," chimed in Godwyn demurely. She was thinking to herself that she should not much care about playing to Mrs. Melksham, who kept time with her head; to Aunt Rachel, who said "Oh, thank you," when the other pieces were concluded, just as if she had been released from prison, and could breathe again freely; or to the Oxford friend, who wore a forced smile, which made his face look like a mask. Nor was she likely to have any appreciation from Humphrey, who stretched out his long limbs lazily, declaring he had not been asleep, but privately voting it all a bore; whilst Christine got through her performance like a machine, or Olive's sharp notes struck on the ear like the thud of bullets.

"My music was all packed in that box," said the little hypocrite.

"As if we had not heard from Fraulein Leibrecht that you were quite independent of your music!" answered Aunt Rachel, who was curious to hear her.

There was nothing more to be said, and Godwyn first played a piece of Mozart's with an exquisite touch and expression which perfectly surprised her auditors, and then, seeing that she had gained their attention, began to improvise with perfect ease, as if she were unconscious, as she probably was by that time, of their existence. Her soul, as

Humphrey said afterwards, seemed to be in her fingers, as, after some difficult passages which showed her command over the instrument, she wound up with a simple air, into which she managed to throw a strange, melancholy plaintiveness.

"Why didn't you tell us you played like *that?*" asked Olive abruptly, as in the pause which followed Godwyn seated herself at a little distance, without seeming to remember that she had caused any emotion.

"I must get that piece for Christine. There was really nothing in the execution, but it is astonishing what elegant things you can get hold of in Germany," added Mrs. Melksham. "You must let me have the name of it."

The musician's lips curved involuntarily, and Humphrey burst into a laugh.

"Tell us the truth," he said. "It is your own—we must really have it published. You have developed a talent for music which is perfectly extraordinary."

"There is nothing at all astonishing in it when anyone has learnt harmony," said the girl, scarcely knowing whether to be pleased or vexed at the little ovation which the two young men seemed to be determined to give her.

"You ought not to run it down; it is a marvellous talent," exclaimed Charlie Duke, in a state of excitement, pressing nearer to her, " and I have no doubt you can sing as well as you can play."

" That depends on whether people like my voice. It goes up a good way, and comes a good way down, but it is always a matter of taste about a voice," she answered, a little amused at seeing him stirred into enthusiasm.

" Sing us something of your own. You must compose something for my violin. There is nothing like these original compositions; there is something novel in the idea of them," added Humphrey, determinedly leading her to the piano.

She sang a little unpretending melody set to touching words, and when she ceased there was silence again in the room. Mrs. Melksham was the first to speak, in an aside to Christine,

" She calls it original, but I am perfectly certain I have heard something like it before."

The girl had tears in her eyes, and turned aside to hide them.

"Whose are the words?" asked Charlie Duke.

"Oh, the words—you ought to know —they are only a translation from Uhland."

"Did I not say the other night she was penning a sonnet to the moon?" laughed Olive, who thought they had been grave enough.

"Nothing will satisfy Uncle James till he has had these things published for you. He will be as proud as Lucifer of them," said Humphrey with decision.

"He will publish them, you mean, at his own expense?" said Godwyn with a sudden flush which rose to her forehead. "Nothing that I have ever written shall be published in *that* way. If I had to get my living by them it would be different. Perhaps some day I may have to ——" She stopped abruptly, and then continued, " Do you really think I would have them published by Uncle James's money, to interfere with the legitimate earnings of other poorer women, when the numbers are so frightfully crowded of those who have to struggle for their daily bread? No. I hope you will not say a word to Uncle James about it. It would pain me to refuse him, but I should have to be firm about it. I don't believe that any one really cares for music who cannot cultivate it for the sake of a private joy. To have an enthusiasm for some occupation, a delight in some pursuit, may be an excellent thing to save us from getting narrow and mean, but to want to display it to all the world just for the sake of showing off ——"

" Humphrey, you have brought a tirade on your head. My dear, are you not making a terrible fuss about nothing?"

said Mrs. Melksham scornfully, as Godwyn, with clasped hands, sparkling eyes,
and flushed cheeks, looked prettier than
she had ever thought it could be possible
for her to look.

" You ought to know human nature
too well to contradict her. I should say
that where Miss Payton is determined
nothing will make her change her mind,"
laughed Charlie Duke, as Aunt Rachel
sagely remarked—

" *I* think she is perfectly right. Young
people often fancy it a very grand thing
to win that sort of triumph, but take my
word for it, it is a very poor triumph—it
generally leads to disappointment."

CHAPTER XII.

THE next few days effected a transformation in Godwyn's appearance. The
" contract," which, as Mr. Bardsley reminded her, she had sealed with a kiss,
sometimes cost more than the few rebuffs
which she had been prepared to meet with
from Mrs. Melksham.

She had secretly rebelled agaiust the
extravagance when her guardian presented her with a twenty-pound note as
her first quarter's allowance, and told
her he expected her to spend the whole of
it on her own adornment. The comfort-

able schoolgirlish toilettes were con-
demned as unwearable, and she was told
that she was expected to dress as expen-
sively as Olive Neale.

" Not that you need carry fashions to
the exaggerations that she does," said
the old man, as he noticed the humorous
expression of her face. " She does more
to distort nature than most women, and
that is saying a good deal. Use your
own good sense, without copying any
one, and please me by dressing in ma-
terials which would be fitting for you if
you were my daughter."

Forced to do as she was directed, without teasing him any further about her
state of puzzle and perturbation, Godwyn,
who had overheard Olive whispering, that
she was " only a poor dependant," and
who would willingly have put off her
elegant attire, appeared, after a few days,

equipped in such excellent taste that Humphrey was tempted to reverse the decision which he had so hastily made when he first saw her.

On the same day when her wardrobe had received its reinforcement, as if he had planned it on purpose, the old man, with a new gallantry which would sometimes tempt him from his solitude, insisted on taking his visitors to see a collection of pictures which he had amassed with considerable care; acting as showman himself, as he walked through the room on the ground-floor —a handsome room with brown oak panuelling — which had been fitted up to receive his favourite art treasures.

" That is my mother's portrait," said Humphrey, joining Godwyn, who had wandered apart from the rest, and was looking at one of the few family portraits.

It was the face of a rosy-lipped, bright-eyed young woman, with sunshine in her face, and a baby in her arms.

" That podgy lump of fat was meant for me. Do you know I just remember her when I was a trifle less podgy? I always think of Cowper's lines when I look at this picture. I wouldn't tell every one, but it reminds me of how I used to talk to you about her as a child, and you used to talk to me, you know, of *your* mother," he added, with a change of feeling in his tone. It was the first time he had, of his own accord, introduced the subject of their childhood.

Just then, Mr. Bardsley, wishing to direct their attention to a picture which he had lately purchased from the walls of the Academy, turned round to look

for the missing couple, and was struck
by his ward's poetical face, and by the
subtle attraction of her graceful carriage,
set off by the plain close-fitting dress,
making the shapely curves of her figure
look like those of a statue as she walked,
with all her pleasing unconsciousness,
past that corner of the room in which
were hung the few portraits of which he
could boast as belonging to his family.
At that moment something recalled to
him the story of the house—how the old
family which had been sheltered beneath
its roof for many generations had been
turned adrift in poverty and debt to seek
a lodging elsewhere.

It had been one of the miseries of his
bachelorhood that he could not found a
new family. But who could tell? Before
he died that new family might be founded.
And who more worthy than Godwyn

Payton to hand down the traditions of the new family? A warm glow came to his heart when he noticed that her eyes were fixed on Humphrey, and that she seemed to have forgotten herself in listening to the words which came from his lips.

" She may not know it—she is too simple—but she loves him still; not a doubt of it," thought the uncle, glad to give his own interpretation to the looks with which she regarded his nephew.

" You have been very much occupied," said Olive, in an affected tone, a minute or two afterwards, when the cavalier whom she usually appropriated took his place by her side.

" I was talking to my cousin."

" Cousin !" she answered sharply : " how is it you are cousins? Second cousin, I suppose, for I never heard that

Mr. Bardsley had more than three sisters, and her name is not either of theirs, nor is it Bardsley, as it would be if he ever had had a brother."

" Had you not better go straight to him for the family history?" said Humphrey, the abrupt question taking him suddenly aback. He could not understand why she questioned him with the same ease as if he had been a girl.

" Oh, you need not look surprised at me if I know more than I tell you; and you mean to say she does not know it. It is not *my* place to enlighten her," she continued, with a smile. " I daresay it is only gossip—the gossip of servants —but it is not *her* fault. She is terribly to be pitied, poor thing!"

Humphrey started and looked at her. He was almost roused from his usual languor into a retort that Olive might

not easily have forgotten, but his experience had taught him to think himself
so popular with women, that he made
excuses for her rudeness by concluding
that she was suffering from a pang of
jealousy. Olive Neale had been endowed
with fair natural faculties, but her cul-
ture was insufficient, her worldliness in-
corrigible, and there were times when
her deficiencies jarred on Humphrey's
finer taste, developed by a certain amount
of education and intellect.

The body was fair enough, if only the
soul were beautiful like it. There had
been times when her coquettish smiles
had seemed to say to him, even before
Godwyn's arrival, " I am ignorant and
narrow—my education has been incom-
plete—but you must admire me all the
same, I am so beautiful—don't you see
how trustful, how confiding I am?" But

now, when she attempted one of her
pretty apologies, her face dimpling into
the usual roguishness with traitorous
curves of her lips as she lisped, " I am
afraid you think I am very giddy, but
my gossip is very harmless—women could
not exist without gossip," he felt the
excuse, with the ridiculous and unnecessary
slur upon her sex, to be absurdly inade-
quate. The only comfort was that Mr.
Bardsley had kept his own counsel, and
that Olive, mischievous as she was, could
not find out much about Godwyn.

CHAPTER XIII.

MANY things might flourish in that easy atmosphere at Dornton manor-house. It was by no means incompatible with kindliness and refinement, taste and gracefulness, but it was not calculated to foster any of the sterner virtues, such as self-denial or self-dependence; and Humphrey, who was endowed with some of the best endowments a man could possibly have, had certainly not troubled himself to make much use of them.

The superabundance of vitality which

had distinguished him in his boyhood seemed to be of little value in his manhood. All the good motives, the benevolent aims, and the high promises which had existed in embryo *then* seemed to have melted away now in an atmosphere of self-indulgence. He could let off his remaining energy in shooting or fishing or in agricultural pursuits; but though he could still dabble in art, and though he had his fair share of literary, poetical, and philosophical thoughts, gathered from books or newspapers, a looker-on might have doubted if he had really much occasion to pride himself on superiority to the girl whose manœuvres had so far prospered that she had every reason for hoping she would secure him, with all his promised wealth, for her husband.

The more Godwyn Payton saw of him the more impossible it was for her to help being annoyed at that strange new indolence of manner which was said by people who flattered him to give "repose" to his movements. His greatest enemy could never accuse him of doing anything hurried or awkward, and his greatest friend could hardly class him as one of lofty views and noble uses.

Godwyn was disappointed with her old playmate. But when her box arrived with her music, she was so much engaged with her piano, and with doing her best to help Christine, who had taken a childish fancy to her, that she took little or no part in what was going on in the house.

Mrs. Melksham remained the virtual mistress, and it was only by hearing the altered tones, soft as the cooing of a turtle dove, which Christine called her mother's "company voice," that the girls guessed when there were visitors in the drawing-room.

For visitors were plentiful. The times had altered. Villas—whose recent origin it was easy to conjecture from the too-dazzling whiteness of the staring stucco—had sprung up within driving distances on the neighbouring coast since Godwyn's absence at Heidelberg, and it was no longer difficult at any time to organise picnics in the deep glens by the seashore, impromptu dances, or lawn-tennis parties.

"You will come with us?" said Aunt Rachel on some of these occasions. And Godwyn, nothing loath to visit her old haunts, joined the

picnics more than once, and would
have found them enjoyable enough
but for the occasional presence of Mr.
Hayden, the prosperous manager, to
whom she had taken such an aversion
as a child. His bargaining and brow-
beating had gone on uninterrupted
since her absence; a long course of
success had made him intolerant of
failure, and he seemed to have grown
more arrogant and officious to his
inferiors and more wheedling to his
employer, pestering her with attentions
which were beyond measure disagreeable
to her.

One afternoon, when the *al fresco*
lunch was concluded, and when the
girls, in Dolly Varden or Gainsborough
hats, were, with their accompanying
cavaliers, disporting themselves by the
sad sea waves, Godwyn, finding herself

freed for once from Mr. Hayden's annoyances, seated herself on a rock, with the tide curling beneath her feet, and gave herself up to the full enjoyment of the scene. She had taken off her hat, and the sunlight in full glare was throwing out the golden lights, hitherto unsuspected, in her rich brown hair.

"In dreamland?" asked a voice near her, and, looking down, she saw Humphrey, who was wading to reach her.

"Take care of your boots," she replied with a laugh.

He seated himself by her and said,

"This is what you like?"

"Yes, this is what I like," she answered, drawing a deep breath of enjoyment.

"How times are altered! We used both of us to be perfectly happy with this sort of thing. But I can't say I care much about the sea now; it takes up so much room, and it gives me the blues."

She never encouraged him to call up reminiscences of the likings they had had in common, but answered, smiling,

"Had you the blues just now? You say little enough generally, but just now at lunch-time you seemed as if it were too much trouble to talk to any one."

"Supposing it was! It may be easy enough to kill time for the next few weeks in this fashion, but how about the next few years? The dear old fellow has been too good to me for me to treat him scurvily, and he says it will unsettle him if I talk of going abroad. But these are humdrum sort of pleasures. They pall on one at the best of times, and I am getting too old for them; it is a wearisome sort of life."

And he discontentedly knocked off a number of limpets from the rock, pounding them with his stick, instead of looking at his companion, whose eyes were gazing far away at the distant sea, and who answered cheerily,

"Haven't you everything that can make life pleasant? It is a luxuriously tasteful sort of life, I think. Whether it is good for either of us is another question, and yet what God sends must be good; there must, in any case, be something to do for Him."

She was trying to hope that in time she should be acclimatised to this new social atmosphere, with its high living and plain thinking, but it was not in her nature to care much about the succulent dainties of such an existence, and in her heart she thought that she and Humphrey had been happier, with a more pure and wholesome happiness, when they had wandered about barefooted, with no one to reprove them, looking for seaweed and shells on these very rocks.

Her downright honesty forced her to speak again, even at the risk of affronting him.

"'Whatever thy hand findeth to do, do it with thy might,'" she repeated almost beneath her breath, carrying out her vein of thought. "That must apply to the pleasures of life as well as to its labours. I daresay that for you and Miss Neale this sort of thing may be wearisome, but for me it is almost too exciting. I have been shut up in a girl's school, and that makes a difference."

He shot an unusual look at her from beneath his eyelashes—a look that might have told her he wanted to see if she had remained as simple and natural as she had been when a little child, and if her earnestness was still free from a suspicion of "cant," also that he did not like this coupling of his name with Olive's. But her eyes were fixed again on the far sea-line watching the gulls which had been wheeling high over the water, and were now black spots against the horizon, and all such glances were wasted on her.

"Your gentle presence among us is a protest against the lazy epicureanism of our lives," he grumbled half to himself; and then continued, as she did not seem to hear him, "I suppose you think if I remain here long enough I shall grow like that fellow Hayden—selfish, priggish, and vain of my unpopularity amongst the untutored population?"

He threw out the hint as if he waited for a disclaimer, but she merely laughed and said,

"Not quite so yellow, I hope."

"Yellow? yes, I believe you," he said, rising discontentedly, "yellow with much luxury, unwholesome food, or perhaps with toiling after a golden goal."

The conversation did not seem to have amused him as much as he expected. It was as if he had suddenly seen his altered self in a mirror held up by friendly hands, and as if he were trying in vain to get away from the sight.

* * * *

Another sort of sight on the lawn at Dornton manor-house was pretty enough, a few evenings afterwards, with Watteau-like groups of women in light summer clothing and artistic toilettes. It was only one of the ordinary lawn-tennis parties, but there was to be dancing afterwards; and Olive, who pricked up her ears, like a racehorse hearing the sounds of the hounds, whenever dancing was proposed, was in one of her best and merriest of humours, looking more picturesque than usual in an aërial maize-coloured costume, with trailing skirts, poppies in her dusky hair, and a white Shetland shawl thrown daintily over her head in the form of a hood.

Godwyn — who, in her vigorous health, took easily to all sports that required well-trained muscles and a quick eye—was being initiated into the mysteries of the game, and was doing her best to cover the mistakes of Christine, who, more nervous than usual, invariably missed the ball whenever her turn came to hit it, and became vague and ungrammatical in her confusion, inquiring "If it's me?" to the horror of her mother.

"You will give me the pleasure of the first waltz with you?" said one of the gentlemen, sauntering up to Godwyn, when Olive, declaring that it was already becoming too cold on the lawn, and that impromptu dances were the most enjoyable things in the world, set the musician, who had been engaged from the neighbouring town, to strike up the inviting dance-music in the house.

"You had better leave me out of the question. I have never properly learnt dancing, and I don't know that the German fashion is just the same as the English," answered Godwyn, excusing herself, and liking to look on at the pretty scene.

They danced in the picture-gallery, which was conveniently situated on the ground-floor, so that the noise was not likely to disturb Mr. Bardsley; and the fair girlish forms, in billowy white or delicately-tinted colours, with other faces still prettier looking down from the picture-frames on them, and with the elder ladies dressed in velvet and ruffling, and the babble of voices and sound of feet on the oaken floor, furnished as much amusement as Godwyn could require. She was as happy as any of them, sitting alone on a distant bench, with the sound of dancing and the clash of music drowning speech, her happiness being increased by the fact that Christine was enjoying herself, and that a tinge of pink was giving a glow of health to the child's usually pale cheek.

"Godwyn—of all people—a wall-flower?" exclaimed Humphrey, who had been stealing covert glances at the solitary seat as he clasped Olive's hands in the intricacies of the Lancers.

"Oh, Godwyn despises dancing; she is 'superior,' you know; if she were a man she would consider female society frivolous, and look down on the weaker vessel," exclaimed Olive, when, the quadrille being over, she had managed, amidst all her numerous partners, to spare Humphrey a promised waltz. He instinctively relaxed his hold on her fingers, and held them so loosely that they almost fell from his touch; but in another instant he had recovered his usual serenity, and she was whirled away in the waltz.

"How beautifully Olive dances! I think she is quite the best dancer in the room," said Godwyn, when Humphrey joined her a few moments afterwards.

"You are the first woman I ever met with who could be enthusiastic about other women," he said, looking at her with the curious expression which she had once or twice before noticed in his face. "Do you *really* admire Olive?"

"I think she is charming—quite a beauty—indeed, I am inclined to admire the majority of your company this evening."

"Bother the company! I wish the people would go."

"That is not in keeping with your usual politeness."

"You have not been constantly at ball and drum, or you would know that you ought to try to pick out the weak points in other people."

"Suppose I begin with *you*—you were dancing just now with as dismal a look in your face as if you were Count Ugolino."

"Don't betray me to Miss Neale."

"Trust me," she answered, shaking her head; "but you ought to have been happy with your partner. As far as I can judge, it must be one of the advantages of dancing that people can choose their own partners, and are not sorted wrongly in couples, like gloves that don't match"

"You will come in to supper with me?"

"I am not hungry, but it will make a diversion," she said, remembering that they would have to pass by the open windows, and she was longing for a deep draught of the night air.

"You are taking nothing," he remarked a few minutes afterwards. "Have some of this salmon and lobster salad."

"I would rather have some bread and butter. Is not that just like a schoolgirl?" she laughed.

"You must educate yourself to our ways. This is the Castle of Indolence, and one of our ways is to eat salmon and lobster salad for supper. You will train yourself to it if you try. Bread and butter is missish. There must be codes of laws for the science of pleasure, when life is devoted entirely to pleasure by the people who have nothing to do."

"Then *I* should not call it pleasure at all. Neither do *you*," she added decisively. "You are not what you appear to be."

"I am what circumstances make me. If I were to confess the whole truth, I might tell you I should be glad enough to get out of this petty round of ideas and sympathies. But what would you have me do? Shut myself up with Uncle Bardsley, and spend my life in translating Horace? No, I cannot study to grow old; I believe in countries like Australia, lands of liberty for man and beast. At one time I had an idea of breaking through these shackles in England, and trying to fit myself for an artist, but soon I was convinced that if ever there

could be such a thing as an exhibition
of rejected pictures, *my* pictures would
attain to the honour of being in that
exhibition. Now I know I have victim-
ised you to a fearful extent by talking such
egotistical stuff."

She coloured deeply, but did not
answer.

She knew that there was nothing more
to be done with him when he began to
talk in this fashion; but she was more
anxious than ever that nothing should
interfere with her own determination to
live out her life of plain straightforward
duty.

"Could I not go to Girton College,
and prepare myself to be a governess?"
she asked Mr. Bardsley coaxingly the
next day, "if you will not let me help
you. I do so dislike an idle life, and
I may—I may have—to help—my father.

If I cannot go to Girton, there is the London Academy of Music. I could make myself more proficient, and I should have something to fall back upon."

It was some time before her meaning dawned upon him. He had become slow of late to assimilate a new idea, and rather slow to marshal those he had already acquired. Yet a little consideration showed him that there was truth in what she said, and it was the grain of truth which he felt to be irritating.

"What becomes of your contract?" he asked bluntly. "It is the duty of every woman to marry. There is no fear of your ever being obliged to go governessing. I don't know who can have put such nonsensical notions into your head. Your mother never wanted to study like men. She was contented with her lot as a woman, and was happy—in her children. A woman's sphere is in the house."

She looked at him in a pained and puzzled manner, and then turned away her face to hide its working. She had known as a child that her mother's life had not been a happy one.

"I don't agree with you," she said softly. "I know people when they are married are not always happy. My mother, as you say, was happy—in her children; but the other babies died. She had only me left. I am afraid I should not be content with that sort of happiness. I would rather have my music."

"How very odd!" he thought, gazing at her. "Music! She can like music well enough to make up her mind not to marry! Well, Humphrey must manage to shake her resolution. But how different she must be from ordinary girls!"

CHAPTER XIV.

FROM that time Godwyn never carried her difficulties to her uncle. Since it was useless to attempt to obtain information about her father, she tried no longer to trouble herself with hopeless conjecture. But the "contract" which was observed more closely than ever, and which resulted in building up a wall of restraint between the two, could not interfere with the earnest zest with which the girl cultivated her favourite art.

She hated mediocrity, and so suspected

her own powers that she feared to attempt some of the new music which she loved so passionately without further instruction, and Mr. Bardsley humoured her so far that he managed to obtain help for her from a choir-master who came from Exeter. Once a week she had a lesson, and became so happy in her consciousness of power when she found beneath her skilful fingers the true interpretation of her enthusiastic dreams, that it was as if she had taken a new lease of happiness and strength.

The parties which went on at Dornton were of little consequence to her; she did not, as Olive said, "despise" them, but the training which she had had at Heidelberg hardly fitted her to understand them. She had neither ambitious vanity nor the desire to please everybody. All the *ruses de guerre* with which Olive was

familiar, all the little secrets of the
initiated, all the nothings which were
great events for the adepts in gossip, all
the allusions, the half-finished sentences,
the scandals, the detraction, which formed
the staple of the small-talk amongst some
of the other girls who visited the manor-
house, were infinitely wearying to her.
She did not know the alphabet of this
new language. But she could enjoy herself in her country rambles, and she
would escape alone, unnoticed, to the
horror of Mrs. Melksham, who no longer
dared to interfere with her, from dread of
Mr. Bardsley.

One morning when the other ladies
were later than usual, and when Godwyn—
who was often up a couple of hours before
the others had risen—had been tempted
by the morning breeze and by the honeyed
warmth at her wide-flung window to

think of wandering in the fields where the early morning sun was evaporating millions of dew spherules from slender threads of gossamer, she went out with her sketch-book, having determined to sketch one of the most picturesque of the neighbouring cottages.

She had forgotten the anxieties which weighed on her when she first came to Dornton; life and animation had returned to her in full force, and the sunlight seemed to be concentrated that morning in her youthful figure as she sprang up the most precipitous pathways on the cliff with the ease and careless grace of healthy, well-used muscles. She could not at once commence her sketch. "Sentimental, like a school-girl," Olive sometimes said she was, and it is true that her passionate inner life sometimes found its outlet in scribbled fragments of verse. Some of those exquisite melodies of thought and feeling which haunt many of the young with their untried capacities for love, and which come to those whom Richter calls the "dumb ones of heaven," as well as to others gifted with the faculty of expressive speech, haunted her as she seated herself to commence her sketch. A goodly life seemed to lie before her, like a field which the Lord had blessed, and as she lingered, pencil in hand, watching the wide expanse of sea beneath her, with the fearless seamews riding up and down upon the billows, a happiness as intense as theirs seemed to be hers.

She had just begun to sketch in the outline of the cottage with its background of rockwork, woods, and water, her attention being entirely concentrated for the time on her drawing, when she was

suddenly struck on the forehead by a
sharp stone, aimed at her by some one
who must have been ambushed behind
the hedge—a child probably; the hedge
was so low that it was impossible for
it to conceal a person of full stature.
The stone had cut the skin near the eye-
brow, and something warm trickled down
her cheek from the temple.

Sick and dizzy as she was for the moment
with the sudden pain, as she put up her
handkerchief to staunch the blood from her
brow, that strange, self-controlled energy
which she had always been able to
summon to her assistance lately, in spite
of being shaken by nervous trembling,
prompted her to follow the child as it
attempted to make its escape and hide
itself in one of the most dilapidated
of the cottages. More like a hovel
it was than a cottage, as, vaulting over

the hedge, in spite of the rents which were inflicted on her garments, and with an agility which few women could have equalled, Godwyn came up with the boy, as he ducked and tried to evade her grasp, finally holding him tightly as he whined in a fright,

"It weren't my fault, it weren't; it were they as set I on to dew it."

"Ay, and it were they as had their desarts—as had sucked the bluud o' the poore," cried a voice shrill with passion, which came from one of a group of women with rough heads and mud-bespattered garments, collected near the door of one of the cottages, who seemed to have lost their gentleness as well as the natural music of their voices in the squalor and dirt to which they had been inured since childhood.

"I telt yew how it 'ud be if yew went

for to attack the leddy; there's the
gent'men as 'll have yew up for it, there's
the p'lice at Knaresbury!" shrieked
another unwomanly voice, as Godwyn,
still confused from the sharpness of
the pain, could distinguish little amidst
the hubbub of sound, the crying and
recriminating, but that these people, in
some mysterious fashion, had intended to
avenge themselves for some fancied wrongs
by attacking a member of Mr. Bardsley's
family.

"What harm has my uncle done you?"
she cried, rather astonished at first at
the shower-bath of philippic which
greeted her ears, but shocked and
wounded at last by the reproaches
which were being heaped upon the family,
and rousing herself loyally to the defence.
"You ought not to speak of my uncle in
that fashion."

"He—he haven't a word to threw at a dawg—proud as Lucifer he be!" said one of the women who seemed to be better educated than the rest, and who busied herself in binding up the tingling graze, stanching the blood with some cold water; "he've money enough, if he chuse to spend it on what's fitting, for they as 'arns it for 'im, but none on us will ever see the colour on it so long as he be livin'. 'Taint for real badness as 'tis with Hayden; out and out hard *he* is upon everybody; 'tis he as grinds us under 'is heels."

Not a muscle of Godwyn's face had moved, and yet the words which they said to each other made her suffer cruelly. For the first time she recognised the depth of the gulf which lay between the manager and his subordinates; for the first time she realised the intensity of the hatred which led to an act of personal violence, directed even at herself.

"The hurt is nothing—it hurts me much more to think you should speak against us," she said, setting her lips together, and determining not to wince, as she caught sight of one or two anxious faces looking at her sympathetically, in spite of the attempt at bravado. "Let us be friends," she added in another moment, as she rose and stood before them, speaking to them with quiet consideration, and trying to ignore the fact that anything had happened to annoy her; "it was only the ignorance of the little fellow; if he were sent to school he would soon know better. I ought to know some of you," she added, looking more closely at the slatternly women and recognising a face or two which had been familiar to her in her childhood. They had grown to know her appearance since her return as she passed to and fro the village, and had sometimes drawn nearer to the windows to look at her trim figure; and the men who caught passing glimpses of her could say nothing in her disfavour except that she belonged to the family of Bardsley, but that in itself was sufficiently condemnatory.

Once when she attempted to renew her acquaintance with one of the women whom she had liked best as a child, the door had been flung to with apparent ungraciousness, and the loud exclamation,

"I don't want none of them tracks."

"I haven't got any," had been God-

wyn's laughing answer, but the door
had still remained closed upon her,
and she had determined to wait her
time. Anything like intrusion into the
houses of the poor had been to her
specially repulsive. She had been content
to tarry in patience, and the time seemed
to have come at last as she followed the
now terrified and blubbering little delin-
quent, to whom the sound of school was
more awful than that of jail. The door
of the cottage was so low that she had
to stoop to enter it, and the light was so
darkened that it was some time before she
recognised a little emaciated child, also
a boy, but younger than the one who had
aimed the stone at her, stretched on a
miserable bed in one corner of the
room. The child lay with his eyes closed,
apparently in the last extremity of
suffering, with a woman stooping over

his pallet, who looked up as Godwyn entered.

The mother, who had been watching by his bed all the night, was so surprised as the lady came suddenly upon her, that half a laugh, half a cry, burst from her with a sound of misery so wild that Godwyn started back alarmed; at the same time one of the older shrews who had followed her, took advantage of her sudden fright to hiss out terrible words. For a moment, Godwyn's eyes fell before the burning gaze of the old woman, whose skin was like wrinkled parchment and her eyes like live coals, and she could not answer the indignant torrent of words, some of which were blasphemous and repulsive; but the next minute she recovered herself and said, fronting the passionate old crone boldly,

"Are you his grandmother? I think, if I remember, you are. I wish you would let me come in and help you in nursing him. I don't think you are adopting the best plan with him now; he will only be weakened in this foul air."

"Let he be, let he die in paace!" said the old woman in a fresh paroxysm of fury; while the younger one, who had lost child after child, and who had been taught to blame Mr. Bardsley for the death of her children, looked at her with a face livid with suppressed agitation, and resented Godwyn's entreaties that she would push a rag from the only window so as to let in a little ventilation. It needed only a brief examination of the child to see that the case was the result of bad nursing and cruel neglect; but when the mother, gaining hope from Godwyn's gentle, encouraging manner, begged her to purchase physic to save him, it was useless to assure her that buckets of physic could not do him any good without healthier arrangements, cleanliness, and fresh air.

Godwyn did what little she could, promising to send milk and nourishment before the evening. Her first idea on leaving the cottage was to call and tell the clergyman, whom she found at his breakfast, and who answered her, when she entreated him to go and see the woman,

"My dear young lady, I think this is a case rather for Mr. Bardsley than for me. I agree with you that there are— hem—hem—certain sanitary precautions, but really I do not feel it is a matter in which I can interfere."

Tell Mr. Bardsley! Godwyn's heart
sank. She knew she could not get him
to listen; that he would refer her to Mr.
Hayden or to Humphrey, and on her
way home she debated the possibility of
getting assistance from either of them.
That money should be spent recklessly
to make the house on the cliff fit for
so many fine ladies and gentlemen, and
that a new mansion should arise, as it
had done, out of comparative chaos,
might have been all very well had the
poorer people been placed in a condition
of comfort. But after the oaths and
bewailings which she had heard, it seemed
to Godwyn as if the sufferings of the
whole human race had taken hold of
her, crying to her for sympathy and
redress.

As she walked back sadly, with bent
head and heavy steps, she thought no

longer of the brightness of the day, but
of the groanings and writhings of lacer-
ated human hearts. The child who lay
suffering in that adjacent cottage was
only one amongst the numbers who had
been neglected in that village. Thinking
so, it was difficult for her to help
severely blaming Mr. Hayden, still more
difficult to help feeling sorrowfully
ashamed for the other man so dear to
her, who had improved his own house,
but never drained those filthy dens, and
more difficult than all to forget the condition of the half-starved wives and toil-
bowed husbands, who were compelled,
under the present regulations, to receive
two out of the nine shillings they earned
a week in sour cider.

Godwyn had known all this before,
but it had never yet come so forcibly
before her.

She felt older and wiser as she returned by the way she came, full of plans for doing good, and of the dawning of a new era for the people of Dornton. She had almost forgotten the handkerchief which bound her forehead, and which was half concealed by her hat, as she entered at once upon the story of what she had seen, making light of her own share in the adventure.

Breakfast was finished, and Olive and Christine, who were lounging, prettily dressed, by the window, discussing their amusements for the day, for the first time seemed to her to have an artificial appearance, as if their lives were spent in a theatre instead of under the arch of heaven, and the existence of the poor were nothing more to them than a rural idyll.

" I do not think your uncle will allow

you to take any more of these wild walks, or to come home in this dishevelled state," said Mrs. Melksham, in whose presence Godwyn—who could not help dropping small rebellious hints which might come into collision with that lady's most cherished theories—had been propounding some of her novel ideas, and who looked upon these plans as only fit occupation for a lunatic.

" Do you mean," asked the girl, more excitedly than usual, as she turned to her so-called aunt, who stood looking marked disapproval, " that no money can be found to help these poor fellows with their families, while thousands go out elsewhere? I am sure—very sure—my uncle will do something for them when their case is properly represented."

" He thinks they are too encroaching already."

" But *Humphrey* would not think so."

"Don't appeal to 'Humphrey!'" cried Olive, mimicking her tone. " Only the other day I heard him saying that sickly, invalid children, and chronic valetudinarians, should be put speedily out of their misery. He would have them treated like horses that have done their work."

" What do you mean?" asked Godwyn with wide-open eyes.

" Don't appeal to me! I shiver, I turn cold, I know I look blue at the thought. It was Mr. Bardsley——"

" Well?"

" He would have them chloroformed and saved from further trouble," said Olive, looking significant, and raising one of her shoulders.

" How horrible!"

"Not horrible at all," said Humphrey, attempting a jocose explanation, yet feeling that he would rather have bitten out his tongue than have made the careless speech which Olive mischievously misinterpreted, and which had driven all the colour out of Godwyn's cheeks. "When society is better organised, every incurable malady will be treated with capital punishment."

She looked at him to see if he were laughing, but Olive was looking at him too, and he continued with apparent gravity,

"Oh, I see you have not studied the progress of the race. If the system of Lycurgus, for instance, were carried out in England, we should do away with hospitals, we should simplify the work of those who recruit for the army, we should be freed from the bother of a whole regiment of doctors, who make the most of our maladies to eke out an uncertain living. But of course we should except women; they should be privileged creatures, and if a woman wished to be freed from her husband, she could find out that he had some incurable malady."

" Why, the world would come to an end!" exclaimed Olive, with a burst of merriment.

" Well, and the new world so long as it lasted could be managed entirely by women. That is the Utopia which the dear creatures wish for at present. Fancy, we should have women in the army, women in the pulpit, women making speeches in Parliament! All the fat ones should drive the omnibuses, and the sharp ones should manage the railways."

" Only banter!" said Godwyn, a little

relieved. Yet why should he treat her with banter when she was so terribly in earnest?

"Well! and a good thing if it *is* banter," responded Olive sharply, "we have had nothing but homilies on the state of the poor ever since you came among us. If we are to talk about nothing but these slow, dry subjects, the least you can do will be to let us get some fun out of them—or else it will really be miserable work."

Godwyn scarcely noticed her sharp speech.

An ungenerous sentiment from Humphrey's lips sounded ten times baser than it would have done from others.

Memory produced another figure, as if in a dream, of the bright-eyed, unselfish boy who had lifted her so tenderly from the window. He had never been so languid then—never joked her then on the sorrows of other people.

" What is a man without work?" she thought to herself. " It is the absence of employment which is ruining him."

In that moment she thought she had outlived the mistaken liking which, in spite of all hindrances, she had hitherto had for him.

CHAPTER XV.

FROM that time Godwyn became more reserved, with the fixed idea of trying to help the poor people at Dornton. Occasionally, since her return to her so-called home, she had had long conversations with her uncle, who had been struck by the breadth of her ideas. He soon found out that she had lived as he had himself, to a certain extent, in a world of her own, loving to poetise, but always laughing at herself for this tendency of hers, and asking pardon for her reveries, which were beautiful when she could be persuaded to repeat them.

But she was now thoroughly emerging from the world of dreams. Lazarus, in the shape of the workman lying at the rich man's gate, if not actually in sores, yet in need of almost everything that is considered necessary for civilised life, had made her even forgetful of her love of music. Yet when, in her attempts to effect a real reform, she made up her mind to speak to Mr. Bardsley, he met her for the first time with an absence of sympathy.

" You take things much too seriously," he said. " Wait till you are my age, dear child, and you will find that all this nervous excitement will never agree with your health."

He waived the subject with a gesture of disgust, as if he were afraid of another discussion, or was disposed, man like, to pooh-pooh her woman's claim to

understand such subjects or to reason
about them, the only result being that
Godwyn, not being forbidden, went on
uninterrupted in her missions of mercy
to the villagers.

She was so untiring in her efforts that
Olive declared she would soon make
herself a great deal worse than the poor
little brat whom she thought it so necessary to nurse. ·

"You make a mistake," said Humphrey in answer. "Country ladies can
accomplish wonders. They are not hothouse flowers, made delicate by luxury :
they——"

"How warm you are about it ! The
country ladies must be obliged to you for
taking up the cudgels in their defence."

"I do not defend them—I only do
them justice," he replied in a dry tone
which made her bite her lips.

" I do not see it can signify to *us*," she answered gaily, " if your cousin is determined to overtax her strength."

" *Us !*" Why did she say " us ?" Somehow the expression grated upon him. As a pleasantry he was quite prepared to laugh at it, but it had a familiar sound which was not quite agreeable to him since Godwyn's improved appearance and superior force of character had dawned upon him more and more.

" We have always been good friends, and I hope we shall never quarrel, but in that case you must abstain from finding fault with my cousin," he answered, in a tone which left her doubtful as to whether he were in earnest or in jest.

That afternoon Godwyn had been sitting for some hours with Mrs. Carslake's grandson, and had braved the old woman,

in spite of the warning which she had
had from one of the neighbours.

"Don't ye—don't ye go near 'em,
Miss; she have a grudge against all the
Bardsleys, Mother Carslake have, and
if ye chanced to offend her, she'd as
lief fly at ye with her teeth as look at
ye."

In defiance of this prophecy, Godwyn,
divesting herself of her cloak and hat,
had aided the overtaxed mother that
day, "jest for all the world," as that
woman remarked, "as if she were as
lowly-like as one o' themselves."

"Let me take him something nice and
pretty from the house," Godwyn had
said on a former occasion, when the boy
had wailed, "Oh! the pain, the pain!"

"'Taint o' no use, Miss," the mother
had answered in a softened mood; "he's
goin' the same as the rest, puur lamb.

He bean't long for this world. I reckon."

But that afternoon a bunch of flowers from the greenhouse and the garden had distracted the child for the first time from the recollection of his suffering, and a pudding, which Godwyn had brought to him in her basket, had tempted him to eat as he had not eaten for weeks.

Godwyn walked back with lightened heart and elastic step, forgetting for the time the existence of Humphrey, who had determined to waylay her in the solitary path up the cliffs, which he knew she would take, and who had speculated a good deal as to what she would think of his unexpected appearance. So little was she thinking of him, that she ran straight against him without seeing him at all, and he could not help being glad that she had left off her schoolgirl's costume, so graceful did she look in her soft-flowing dove-coloured dress.

The dress, a little severe, suited the pale face of the wearer, the expression of which was slightly melancholy, and gave her an air of distinction. She was " really pretty so," he found himself thinking as he looked at her, " pale" as he had called her, after the first day of her arrival, but fair, sensitive and thoughtful-eyed. She was not sallow, as she had been when a child. The skin, like the creamy colour of the magnolia, would bear any inspection, even that of the downright sun, searching ruthlessly for the weakest places.

" Why did you come to meet me— alone ?" she asked meaningly, after the first laugh caused by the sudden- ness of the collision.

" Because two is company, and three

is trumpery," he answered in his old schoolboy fashion, and she found the jollity of the tone catching.

"Why have *you* avoided me so much lately?" he asked in his turn, looking with admiration at the little head with its compact hair, which was as neat and clean as a bird's. "It is rather hard that you should waste all your prettiness on these unappreciative cottagers."

"They are not unappreciative," she answered, aware that he was looking at her with approving eyes, but not letting the least trace of feeling of any kind pass over her undisturbed countenance. "I do not care for too great a show of gratitude."

He had placed her arm within his and was looking at her again, but she averted the eyes which he was just

thinking were so far-seeing and full of
solemnity, so shy and modest, but
quick to find out what was wrong,
that they might see as plainly through
any one as if she were looking
through glass. She averted them perhaps purposely, and he was a little
mortified to think that she could not
notice the look of admiration which
passed over his face, and that
it was a pity she was not aware
of it.

"Your best friends wish you would
not wear yourself out with these
constant visits to the village," he
said presently; and she answered, with
a quick smile,

"It does not wear me out—it
does me all the good in the world."

"Is not this zeal rather exagger-
ated?"

" Everything may be exaggeration, carried to absurdity; but I never could see that the possibility of exaggeration furnished a logical argument against the thing in moderation," she answered him in his own serio-comic fashion.

"Did you ever study Kant or Fichte when you were in Germany? Aunt Laura would not call it moderation for young ladies to wander about by themselves in this fashion."

"Do you mean to reproach me or make fun of me? That is not right of you; I am not a young lady, and I know all about the place, much better than Aunt Laura."

"I don't mean to reproach you, but I mean to look after you occasionally; I mean to come and meet you generally when it is late in the afternoon. Does that please you?"

She did not answer.

" If the term 'young lady' does not please you, you are a young woman, and a good-looking one."

She coloured and replied that she was not good-looking, and that she hated compliments, and wished he would not pay them to her.

" So good as you are, and sensible," he answered, a little nettled, " I don't see why you should be disturbed by my telling you the plain truth. If you are beautiful it is God who has given you your beauty—so you would remind me yourself—He who has showered it with such a bountiful hand over the universe."

He spoke with a shade of em-

barrassment which she did not understand, so accustomed was she to
think that Olive Neale had eclisped
her. But by this time she had taken
herself to task for having shown any
annoyance at his pretty speech—
as if the compliment of a brother
should have scandalised and frightened
her !

It seemed like a last opportunity
to seek for the open-hearted companion
of former years, and she determined
to use it.

" Humphrey," she said suddenly, " I
wish you would not only meet me, but
sometimes accompany me in these
walks, try to know these people more
familiarly, visit them, and help them.
Just now when you were making a
kind speech to me you used a holy
name which these workpeople scarcely

know; they live like downright heathens. Humphrey, it is partly *your* fault."

"You see what strange ideas you take into your absurd little head. Have I not reason to laugh at you? I do believe you think I could be doctor and parson rolled into one, and be personally responsible for the bodies and souls of all these scamps. What a romantic idea!"

"You may say what you like, it is no idea. I am not romantic—it is the sober truth."

The contrast between the intense earnestness of her face and the easy superficiality of his was almost startling at that moment. It was characteristic of him that he did not like needlessly to hurt her feelings, and answered in a mollifying tone,

"I like to *see* industrious people, though I am not much given that way myself."

"I take no credit to myself for what you call industry—it is my nature. I think I am not happy in idleness," she answered a little sadly; "but the worst of it is we women cannot work like men—we feel things more sharply because we cannot *do*. Humphrey, don't you think that a man born to wealth ought to doubt his moral title to it, till he has learnt to diffuse some blessings around him?" She had meditated about the speech before she made it, or it would not have been so carefully worded.

"I confess I don't understand you," he said, after a pause, during which it had chilled her to see the gradual lengthening of his face; "you must expect me to be quite unprepared for such high-wrought sentiment."

" Don't you," she said, hesitatingly at first, and then with an enthusiasm which took away her reserve, and lit up her great, earnest eyes—" don't you think that whereas I, who am a nobody, am helpless, you can help effectually? Don't you think it will be your fault, as you are the heir, if these people continue to sink, and that it is your duty to try and raise them ?"

" Upon my word !" he said beneath his breath, as he turned away from the eloquent, innocent eyes which seemed to upbraid him so unnecessarily, his rooted dislike to any kind of effort making this continuous appeal to him decidedly offensive.

" Ah !—coffee-rooms,   reading-rooms,

night-schools, and all that kind of humbug for making a pet of the working-man, you mean, I suppose," he said aloud. "I should like to see Hayden's face if I came out in that line. I daresay you would like me to patrol the whole district, see that the lights are put out by a sort of curfew bell, and revive the lord and serf feeling of the Middle Ages."

"If you are going to turn the thing into ridicule," she faltered, letting go his arm, and then unconsciously putting out her hands as if feeling for a prop —for there was slippery grass at the edge of the cliff, and in her excitement she nearly missed her footing.

He smiled slightly, but did not again offer her his arm.

"Why, you are as grave as if arguing the case before judge and jury."

"It is enough to make me grave when I find you leaving everything to Mr. Hayden, and always believing everything you hear. It is absurd for you with your secure income to expect perfection from those who live from hand to mouth."

"Do you mean to say that Hayden is not the man we think him?"

"Who knows?

"Who knows indeed? Continued speculation about matters on which one has not the slightest information is rather likely to stultify the intellect. I should think it is far wiser to let things go," he continued, lazily as ever. She stopped short and looked at him—at his strong, finely-formed hands, his capable figure, and his languid face—with the eyes which, a few minutes before, he had thought of as being shy, modest, and yet as capable of seeing through a fellow as if she were looking through glass, and said, speaking clearly, almost sharply, with passionate earnestness,

"Why are you so altered? You used not to be indolent and apathetic when you were a boy. What is this change that has come over you? Is it always to be the 'Let us alone' like the lotus eaters? Humphrey, it is of *you*, as well as of the people, that I am thinking. It would be better that you should not inherit one farthing of this money than that you should let the money eat the heart of you, and ruin your manhood."

She put up her hands to wipe the

tears which indignation and wretched-
ness had brought to her eyes. She
was ashamed as soon as she had
spoken, but her passionate impulse had
communicated itself to him like the
sudden spreading of fire. Her lips parted
as if she were still speaking, but at first
he could not answer a word. The trans-
mission of her energy had surprised him,
and there was an unusual gleam of
light in his eyes, ready to kindle into
flame, as he turned round, and in his
turn averted his face, all his pulses tingling with excitement.

Good heavens! could he ever have
been accused of indolence and apathy,
and that by the woman whom now he
knew that he loved a thousand times more
than all the fashionable beauties whom
he had seen, and pretended to love,
since she left England? The necessity

for some sort of speech struck him with urgent force, and he spoke at last, breaking the uncomfortable pause,

"So," he said, trying to laugh, "you mean to give the other women a handle when they tell me that we have caught a tartar? It is new for you to come out in the character of a shrew. If I did not answer you at once it is because, as Johnson said to Boswell, 'I had nothing ready, sir.' Changed?—yes, of course I am changed. I am three years older than you, and you can't expect me to take my cue from you in everything. Remember, I have to deal with such a man as my uncle, who thinks me well enough when I keep the place he has assigned to me, but who cannot away with new theories, and who is always pooh-poohing the new-fangled notions of the rising generation. What did well enough for our fathers he thinks does well enough for us still; you must have heard him say that there will always be helots in the world, and that only fools rave about raising the masses. You don't know how hard it is for a man to be placed in such a position as I am. I have never been brought up to understand anything at all about the business; all the management of the profits, et cetera, has been left to Hayden, and the thing seems to prosper under his management. I must say it seemed scarcely fair to me at first to be kept in such darkness, but now I loathe the whole affair, and these squalid people are horrible to me. My life is of necessity the life of a man who, having failed to choose his natural vocation, must perforce undertake something else chosen for him."

He spoke rapidly, driven, as he felt, to take the worst part of the argument; but she answered as rapidly,

"You can't reason in that way—you can't be crushed by your own fate; it is everyone's duty to conquer circumstances."

"Nonsense!" he said, becoming angry in his self-defence. "There are irreversible laws in the moral and spiritual world, just as there are in the physical."

"Oh, but the laws can be conquered. We can defy the lightning by a simple conductor, and it will play innocently round us. Where we have obeyed the conditions of Nature there Nature is on our side," she answered, her composure breaking down a little again, in quicker and sharper tones. "Why, Humphrey, you can be like the engineer, who can throw bridges over torrents called impracticable, and pierce the mountains when he chooses. I don't believe in 'irreversible' laws. If man was intended to study evil it was in order to conquer it. That is the nearest solution I have ever found to the problem of why God permitted evil."

She stopped again, waiting for an answer, and he turned the face which for the last few minutes he had been carefully averting.

"It was a great mistake," he said, "to keep you at school beyond the proper time, and make a learned woman of you. Go on. I am ready to listen."

But there was a dead silence—on her part a dismayed and lily-cheeked silence. She made an involuntary movement as if she regretted her confidence, and hastened on in nervous shame at the thought of having said too much. The sun sank lower and lower after they had lapsed into that silence. The light became uncertain, and she struck her foot more than once against a stone as she hurried on in that new nervousness.

"You had better take my hand," he suggested at last.

But though she suffered him to take the hand, the touch of which thrilled him as if by an electric shock, she was scarcely conscious that he held it with an unusually hard grip.

"Thank you," he said as they parted at the door of the house. "I will think of what you have said."

But the words of scorn still lingered in her ears. And though he said

" Thank you," it seemed to her that he spoke in a hard, repulsing manner.

END OF THE FIRST VOLUME.

London : Printed by A. Schulze, 13, Poland Street.